ESCAPE

Frost had only the doctor's word that this hospital—if it really was a hospital—was in Moscow. Frost had the papers of the guard whose uniform he'd taken, but the face looked nothing like his own. And if anyone asked him a question, he wouldn't have the right words to answer with.

Frost put his hand on the doorknob. Slowly, he opened the door and stepped into the hallway. Walking confidently toward the glass door, Frost prepared to snap the butt of his AKM into the jaw of the guard who stood there. Frost jammed the guard swiftly. The guard's head snapped back and his body slumped against the wall.

There were two buttons beside the guard, one green and one red. If Frost guessed his Russian security right, the red button would open the glass door. He pressed the button, heard a buzz and a click. But the door locked again before he could pass through. "Hmm," he murmured, then looked to the guard's limp body for a weight. He bent over the unconscious soldier and hefted the body against the red button. The door latch clicked again, allowing Frost to pass through.

Glancing behind him, Frost could see the guard starting to awaken, smothering the other button under his shifted weight.

The halls filled with a deafening alarm . . . .

THE CONTINUING MERCENARY SERIES
BY AXEL KILGORE

#8: ASSASSIN'S EXPRESS (955, $2.50)
Intrigue at every curve. That's what Frost finds while driving a sultry undercover agent from Los Angeles to Washington, D.C. But someone wants them off the road, and Frost has to find out why!

#9: THE TERROR CONTRACT (985, $2.50)
Frost follows a bloody trail of killings and kidnappings when he infiltrates a global terror network. His aim: to seek revenge on the gang that killed his woman!

#10: BUSH WARFARE (1023, $2.50)
Hijacked in Africa, Frost awakens in a jungle and finds himself poisoned by a deadly woman. After he gets the antidote—he plans to give her a taste of her own medicine!

#11: DEATH LUST! (1056, $2.50)
Frost is trailing the treacherous Eva Chapman, a munitions runner who has enough weapons to field an army. He vows to killer her—before she plunges the world into nuclear war!

#12: HEADSHOT! (1129, $2.50)
As Frost fights against Castro death squads, M-19 guerillas, and professional hitmen, it's hard for him to figure if the fiery beauty who hired him wants him more as a lover—or as a target!

#13: NAKED BLADE, NAKED GUN (1162, $2.50)
When the merc runs into an old adversary—who blew away his C.O. back in 'Nam—he's on a trail that leads to the murderously eager arms of a group of religious fanatics—being run from Moscow!

ZEBRA BOOKS
KENSINGTON PUBLISHING CORP.

ZEBRA BOOKS

are published by

KENSINGTON PUBLISHING CORP.
475 Park Avenue South
New York, N.Y. 10016

Printed in the United States of America

For Paul and Mary Lou—good friends,
then and now—all the best . . .

Chapter One

Hank Frost wondered if boredom could be fatal. He loved Bess, and living with her had in some ways been the happiest time of his life. Boredom with Bess would be impossible for him; but he was bored with the other things. He had practiced shooting so much that he had cut a half-inch off his best group size with the Metalifed Browning High Power. He had invested in other guns, and practiced shooting these as well. He had seen every movie release that had sounded remotely promising, averaged reading three books per week. The time was fast coming, he knew, when something to do, something to engage his attention, his mind, his energies, would have to come along—fast. There had been no mercenary contracts coming his way, and even if there had been, he wondered how he'd be able to rationalize accepting one when he had a million dollars in various banks and was living off the interest. No contract could pay what he already made.

Had money corrupted, he wondered—corrupted his life?

The one-eyed man felt himself begin to smile, then heard himself laugh—the laughter loud like that of a lunatic in the otherwise total stillness of the forest.

What could possibly corrupt him?

His laughter subsided. The stillness again. Georgia woods were like that, he had learned, sometimes so totally still it would not have been difficult to convince oneself everything else that lived in the world had stopped living, was somehow gone.

He shook his head, mentally and physically shrugging, snatching a Camel from the half-emptied, partially crumpled package in the right outside pocket of his windbreaker. He found his lighter, flicking back the cowling, rolling the striking wheel under his thumb, then poking the tip of the Camel into the battered Zippo's blue-yellow flame. He snapped the lighter closed with an audible click, then pocketed it. He inhaled the smoke deep into his lungs, then picked up the Barnett Commando Crossbow from the stump beside him.

"Hmmm," he murmured. He had fired crossbows occasionally in Viet Nam while in Special Forces, but nothing quite like this crossbow. He had seen one in a movie, seen one in a store, and finally decided to buy one.

"Here goes," he said with a shrug.

The toe of the crossbow against the ground just in front of his feet, his right knee slightly braced against the break in the frame, he applied downward pressure on the hook at the toe of the skeletonized stock's butt and broke open the piece, the action cocking the prod and automatically setting the safety.

Frost hefted the crossbow in his hands, then drew a field point bolt from the leather quiver at his belt, setting the bolt in the flight groove. You didn't nock the bolts on the string—the string just moved against the flat base of the shaft. He double checked the position of the fletching (the plastic feathers) and raised the stock to his shoulder. He had placed an A-14 hundred-yard small-bore rifle target a hundred yards out with an adequate red Georgia clay backstop behind it. He settled the Commando's front post into the rear notch, then with his right thumb moved the safety into the firing position, then cheeked down, his trigger finger still along the receiver—at least he would have called it that in a rifle.

He moved the finger against the trigger, then whished off. No recoil, only a slight drawing forward, a whoosh, a twang—and the 175-pound draw was expended.

He lowered the Barnett Commando. "Son of a gun," the one-eyed man murmured. He had hit either the "ten" or the "x" ring—he couldn't quite tell.

Frost looked at the crossbow in his hands. "Damn fine," he murmured. Frost started walking, downrange, to confirm the exact spot of the hit.

The one-eyed man stopped.

The silence—it was suddenly gone. A deer would have known better than to come that close to a clearing with a man moving through it, or at any event a deer wouldn't have made that much noise. Frost continued moving, approaching the target—it wasn't the "x" ring, but only a "ten"—not bad, he thought absently, his right hand moving slowly under his windbreaker, breaking the thumb snap on the Cobra Comvest shoulder rig, his fist tightening around the Pachmayr-gripped butt of the automatic.

He stopped in front of the target, the sound of leaves being crushed under heavy footfalls coming up behind him.

The one-eyed man wheeled, the crossbow still in his left hand, his right hand arcing from under his jacket, the right thumb jacking back the hammer of the Metalifed Browning High Power, the first finger of his right hand easing into the trigger guard as the gun came up, the front of the slide settling on the chest of a man running toward him. Behind him were three other men, all of them armed with handguns of varying descriptions. Frost's finger pumped the trigger—once, then again, the 115-grain JHPs slamming into the lead man's center of mass, the body spinning, tumbling backward into the man behind him, the pistol in the man's hands discharging into the ground as he fell. Frost swung the pistol left, into the third man, firing again, a fast two-shot semi-automatic burst—a clean miss. Frost started to drop the crossbow, to steady the pistol with his left hand. There was a sound behind him and Frost side-stepped left and wheeled, the crossbow dropped now, the muzzle of the High Power coming up. Two men came at him over the lip of the red clay enbankment where he'd set his target. The first man dove from the top of the mound, Frost's pistol bucking twice in his bunched fists, the man's body starting to roll in mid-air, then dropping. Frost felt something hammer at his legs—he was going down and he twisted his body to the left as his legs went from under him. . . .

The blurred shape of a man in dark clothes—the third man he'd missed before?

Frost couldn't get the High Power down to shoot; instead he smashed the butt down hard across the back of the man's shoulders as they hit the dirt. There was a groan, and Frost raised the pistol, then hammered it down again, feeling other hands reaching for him. The arms around his legs loosened. Frost, rolling, punched the High Power up and out in his right fist, the muzzle inches away from a face he'd never seen before. Frost pumped the High Power's trigger once, then again. The strange face exploded.

The one-eyed man was up to his knees, a foot snapping out toward him, his right wrist numbed for an instant, then pain—the pistol was gone. Frost dove forward, snatching at the crossbow, rolling, another face looming over him— a gun that looked more like a toy than a real gun was aimed at him. Frost snapped the hooked butt of the Barnett Commando up and out, the hook catching at the left side of the man's face, knocking him back. The weird pistol discharged with a hiccuping sound. Frost shot a glance to the ground beside him. He saw a dart. Where had it come from?

The one-eyed man was to his feet, his left foot snaking out, catching at the tip of the jaw of another man. Where were they coming from? Frost wondered.

He hadn't counted that many.

He wheeled, raking the butt of the Commando out again, the target face sidestepping above the body that owned it. Frost's right foot snapped out as he wheeled half left, a double Tae Kwon Do kick into the chest and upper abdomen. The man fell back.

Frost saw an opening and started to run. He saw a figure coming at him from the trees. His left hand snatched at the little Gerber knife he carried inside his trouser band, grasping the catspaw-surfaced handle. His left arm swung out, underhanding the knife up and out, the pistol in the target man's right hand raising up, the knife hammering into the chest. The man's body sagged as if the knife weighed a thousand pounds; then the man fell.

Frost kept running, out of the open field now, into the trees.

He wheeled, hearing a sound behind him, the man making the sound ten yards to his right. Frost instinctively dodged, a dart punching into the Georgia pine trunk two inches from his right arm.

Frost punched the nosepiece of the Commando down into the dirt at his feet, kneed against the break, and cocked the crossbow. He snapped it closed, snatching a bolt from his quiver and setting it into the flight groove.

He shouldered the weapon, his thumb wiping off the safety, his right finger twitching against the trigger. There was a whooshing sound, a twang. The gunman's hand went to his chest, the bolt sticking out of the white shirt front, and the man fell back.

Frost cocked the crossbow again, then started to run, inserting a bolt into the flight groove as he dodged tree trunks. He heard the shouts of running men behind him. He wheeled the safety already off, holding the Barnett Commando at the hip, then pumped the trigger, the bolt flying. A scream ripped from the lead man as the bolt homed into the belt line, then a series of almost animal cries as the man rolled on the ground.

Frost wheeled to run again, another face looming up in front of him. Frost snapped the hooked butt of the Commando up and out—one more face gone.

He kept moving, hearing the sound of running feet to his left, wheeling. Then three men lunged for him. The butt of the crossbow hammered away one face, but a healthy-sized fist hammered into Frost's jaw. The one-eyed man rolled back with the punch, hands wrestling the crossbow from his own hands.

Frost's left hooked up as he recovered, snapping out, finding the right side of the face of the man with the fist. The one-eyed man could feel the skin of his knuckles split against bone, hearing the groaning sound, feel the rush of air on his face—the man had been eating garlic.

Frost started to turn, two men blocking him. His right hand snaked down to the bolt quiver at his belt, snatching out one of the field points. Then, holding it like a dagger by the shaft, he hammered it into the chest of the nearest man, killing him.

Frost snatched at another of the bolts, slashing with it as the second man dove at him. Frost punctured the neck, the man screaming horribly. The one-eyed man kept running.

Who the hell are these guys? Frost thought. He kept running, hearing the man behind him.

His car—the LTD—was beyond the woods. The KG-99 assault pistol was in the trunk. If only—

He heard a popping sound—like a loud hiccup—then felt something like a needle in the back of his neck.

He swatted at it, like a fly, finding the dart, wrenching it out, stumbling forward, feeling suddenly nauseous. But Frost tried to run, stumbling again, lurching into a tree trunk.

He fell against it. Hands reached out to him. The one-eyed man stabbed another of the bolts outward, into an arm. Recovering, he stabbed at a chest, missing, then stabbed again.

There was a scream and Frost pushed himself away from the tree, tried to run.

Hank Frost fell forward onto his face—he saw the leaves and matted pine needles smashing up toward his face as he closed his eye. . . .

Chapter Two

Frost opened his eye—his vision was blurred and he made to move his right hand to rub the eye. The hand didn't move. He tried the left hand—it didn't move either.

"Shit," he murmured, trying to roll over. He couldn't roll over. He squinted his right eye tightly and opened it again. His vision was blurry, but not quite as much as before. A white ceiling—a bad paint job. He squinted again, then looked down along the length of his body. He was wearing white—his old white suit? It looked more like Bess's night gown— or a hospital gown? He could see his knee caps, one of them bruised. He was wearing a hospital gown.

He tried to move his hands again—then looked at his wrists. There were heavy leather straps confining his wrists. He strained to raise his head. His neck ached and so did his back as he moved. He could barely make out his bare ankles—bare except for the leather straps around them.

He had to urinate.

"Hospital?" Frost murmured. His tongue felt thick, his lips dry, his mouth bad tasting. "Too many cigarettes," he mused. He tried to roll over again.

"Straps," he rasped.

A hospital. A hospital gown. Restraint straps. He couldn't remember why he was there. There'd been the fight with those lunatics in the woods and—he closed his eye tightly trying to remember. He thought he remembered a long ride and an ambulance and being very cold and lying in bed. But it wasn't a bed, more like a cart. A hospital gurney?

Frost was suddenly afraid—was this a mental hospital?

He had to urinate. He heard himself shouting, "Hey—I gotta go to the bathroom—somebody!"

He waited, holding his breath. There was no answer. He looked at the walls of the room. Heavy tiles, stained dark in spots—blood?—covered the walls. Soundproofing.

"Hey—I gotta piss!" There was something wrong with him—he wasn't acting the way he normally acted, he realized. "Hey—hey!"

Logic told him that yelling would serve no purpose, since the walls were evidently soundproofed. "Hey!" But he was still calling out. It was as if his brain were functioning on two levels—one sane and the other—

"Hey!"

Frost fought to calm himself, to get control, his eye scanning his body. The inside of his left forearm was bruised badly, some of the bruises dark and fresh, some yellow and old, a scab visible in one.

"Injections," he murmured.

His kidneys ached and his head was aching worse. He started to shout. "He—" He kept himself from shouting. There was a medicine cabinet, the old, white, high-standing kind that looked like a spray-painted curio cabinet. It was glass fronted and inside it were vials and jars and packages. He could see the lettering on what appeared to be a box of cotton. The letters were in

Cyrllic notation. "Russian," the one-eyed man gasped. . . .

The English was bad, broken but understandable. The man—more the size of a bear—held what looked like a stainless steel cup. It was large, odd-shaped. He was saying, "In this urinate."

Frost opened his eye again, after squinting tightly, looking again at the man and at the cup. He nodded, feeling awkward that he couldn't hold himself while he did it. He filled the cup, then rasped, "Again."

The bear-sized man only nodded, walked out of Frost's peripheral vision to the right, then returned after a moment. The sound of a tank flushing was audible from the far side of the room. Frost worked at filling the cup again. "Thank you," the one-eyed man nodded, saying the words sincerely.

"We go," the big man said, undoing the straps on Frost's wrists. Frost debated. There was a woman standing beside the door—a big woman, more the size of a tall, well-built man—noticeable as a woman only because of her white dress. Awkwardly, the man helping him, Frost sat up. The woman handed the man something that looked like a short white coat.

"Arms in here," the man said.

It was a straitjacket. Frost started to reach for the man, but a hand grasped at his throat, squeezing it at the adam's apple. Frost's feet couldn't move, strapped down still. Frost's hands went to the hand at his throat, tried prying at the fingers. He felt his consciousness going—gone. . . .

Frost could roll over, and as he did he fell hard to the concrete floor beside the high cot on which he had been. His nose ached, as did the side of his head. He tried to touch his nose to see if it were broken. His arms didn't move. He looked down at himself, rolling over. He could feel the concrete under his bare rear-end, the hospital gown up past his hips, his body naked below it. His arms were bound in the straitjacket. But he could think clearly.

He struggled to get to his knees, falling forward onto his arms and left shoulder, throwing his weight against his back to straighten, his back aching. Cautiously, he moved his right leg, then his left—then he stood up.

The one-eyed man fell back, against the edge of the cot-like high bed, his back hurting again as he made contact with the frame. He lurched forward, balancing himself into a standing position. His mind raced. They had intentionally subdued him without giving him a shot—that meant a test, and he needed to be clear headed for the test. Shuffling his feet—stiff and weak in the knees—Frost staggered toward the medicine cabinet. The words were in Russian on the boxes and bottles there. He couldn't read Russian, but had seen enough of it to recognize it.

"Russia?"

Perhaps, the one-eyed man thought, someone was just trying to make him think he was in Russia. There were no windows in the room. No way to tell his surroundings. Frost studied the medicine cabinet again. Even if his hands had been free, there was nothing in the medicine cabinet to use as a weapon.

He was feeling his strength gradually coming back. Turning awkwardly, Frost walked back to the gurney-like bed, leaning against it and working at the confining straps of the straitjacket. It hadn't been hastily put on—it was secure, completely, the one-eyed man realized. "Dammit," he rasped, exhaling a long hard sigh.

He heard the sound of a locking mechanism and turned to his left as the door opened. It was the bear-sized man and the unfeminine nurse.

"Come," the man murmured.

Frost gave him a smile, then asked, "What if I don't? You make me unconscious again it'll ball up your tests."

He realized when he said it that he shouldn't have said it. The man had surprisingly long arms, the left fist hooking out and down and just below Frost's restrained arms, into his gut.

The one-eyed man dropped to his knees, his breath coming hard, vomit rising in his throat.

Coughing, Frost looked up, murmuring, "Bite my ass."

The bear-sized man just laughed, hauling Frost up. Frost felt one of the hands at the back of the straitjacket, the other knotted into his hair. His head cocked back, the man propelled him through the door and into the hallway, Frost slamming against the corridor wall. The beefy nurse caught him and kept him from falling. She didn't smile.

She nodded, and Frost shrugged, walking beside her down the corridor.

The corridor twisted and turned several times, Frost trying to memorize the convolutions.

They stopped then, before an anonymous-looking white door. The bear-sized man opened it and shoved Frost inside. The one-eyed man fell to his bare knees and skidding across the floor. "Eat it," Frost smiled. Then the smile faded. In the center of the room was something that looked like pictures Frost had seen of an electric chair. . . .

The one-eyed man started to pass out, the only sound in the room the sound of his own breathing and a regular, rhythmical electric hum. As his eye closed, he could feel the electric shock starting, hear himself screaming, then shouting, "I'm awake!" The electric shock cut off.

He could not slump his head forward, or back. A skeletonized steel helmet was locked over his head, wire leads running from it—like the leads stuck to his chest, his scrotum and his temples—with some kind of adhesive or glue.

Though he couldn't see his feet, he could feel similar leads attached to his legs, his feet. They were not trying to electrocute him, but rather monitor him, he vaguely realized. And the procedure had endured for what already seemed like hours.

Too weak, too exhausted, too tired, too much so to fight, Frost let them take him back to his room. He was allowed to stand up and piss into a regular urinal this time, making a bit of a mess. Then he was turned around and walked back toward the cot. It looked almost comfortable. He was sat down on the edge of the bed, then rocked around, his legs drawn out, his ankles bound with the leather straps, then the straitjacket loosened behind him. The bear-like man grinned, but Frost didn't try anything. His arms were too stiff to move, the pain of the big man moving them down at his sides making Frost scream involuntarily as the muscles twisted and wrenched. . . .

Chapter Three

There had been a needle, a hypodermic—Frost remembered that, and then an awakening what seemed like seconds afterward. The man and the woman were throwing him into an ice-cold shower. Frost skidded on his bare feet, falling, hitting his head on the cement, then he was hauled to his feet by the bear-sized man. Frost's only consolation had been getting the big man wet in the shower.

His right arm had been twisted behind him, the female nurse helping get the straitjacket on the left arm. Then Frost had felt the bear-sized man's fist balled into his hair again, his head snapped back. Then his right arm was twisted down and put into the straitjacket. The hospital gown had been cold, Frost remembered, cold because his body hadn't really been dry when it had been put on him, much like the straitjacket. They had shuffled down the corridor again; he had been put into the chair and the electrodes attached again. As long as he stayed awake, there had been no pain. He had fallen asleep three times that he could remember—and there had been terrible pain then.

Frost sat there, concentrating in order to keep himself awake and prevent the electric shocks. "I hate you. I hate you. I'll disembowel you with a dull, rusty knife. I'll rip your nose off your face, make you swallow your teeth. I'll stomp on your testicles with spikes—I'll—" He kept at it, telling himself to hate the people who were doing this to him, to live for that, for the hate. He forced all thoughts of Bess, all thoughts of friends like Mike O'Hara out of his mind. Hate and revenge—that would keep him alive. And resentment—authority had always been something he loathed, distrusted—and now authority was doing this to him, making him endure this hell of wakefulness, the pain, the debasement.

The one-eyed man—his eyepatch lost somewhere—sat in the chair, feeling himself looking at once stupid, ugly and helpless. The first two things, he laughed—they were habitual. The third state he would rectify. It wasn't an "if", but a when.

The lights in the darkened room flicked on. The electrodes were removed by the big man, the nurse helping him.

"Up," the bear-like man nodded.

"Up—your ass," Frost smiled. The bear-sized man wrenched Frost to his feet, one of the straps still secured on Frost's wrist, the chair moving, starting to fall, Frost who could barely stand at all, falling with it.

There was a slap across his face. Frost felt blood in the side of his mouth beside his right cheek. Before he could react, the straitjacket was put on him, the female nurse holding her gunboat sized, white-shod foot over his throat.

The man wrenched Frost to his feet, Frost stumbling forward as the arms of the jacket were twisted back, buckled secure and he was shoved ahead. Frost smashed into the door, his face hurting. The one-eyed man summoned all his energy, all he had left. His bare left foot snaked up and out, into the face of the bearsized man. Frost missed the nose, missed breaking it and driving it up through the brain and killing the man. He connected with the teeth instead. Frost slumped back, the big man screaming like a woman would scream, blood gushing from the cracked lips, a tooth protruding through the lower lip.

The bear's hands reached out, grabbing Frost by the neck, the right fist—the size of a Polish ham still in the can—hauling back.

"Nyet!"

The voice was mechanical, perhaps because of the speaker. It was human though, the first voice he'd heard in many days besides his own and the voices of his wardens.

The fist stopped, the bear-sized man's shoulder sagging. The hand reached down and hauled Frost to his feet, the hands covered with blood. "Go," the mumbled words came, and Frost—knowing when he had a good thing—went. The female was the only one with him now. But his energy was gone and he could barely shuffle, let alone fight her. She was bigger than he was, and almost as big as the injured man. Frost felt himself smiling—despite it all—as he looked at the bear-sized man with the missing teeth.

Frost stopped. The woman shoved him ahead. They had turned the wrong way in the corridor. He started to say something. "We're going the wrong—" She didn't speak English anyway, he had decided.

"Go," she murmured, apparently echoing the bear.

Frost shrugged as best he could in the straitjacket and went. The walk went on, seemingly interminably, stopping finally at a door identical to the one behind which lay the electrodes and the chair. "Naw," Frost began.

The woman knocked at the door, then without waiting, opened it, shoving Frost in ahead of her.

There was a window. Frost was enraptured by it, snow

falling past the bars, and the sounds of traffic from the outside. In front of the window sat a man. The man was slightly built from what Frost could see, a high forehead, close-cropped thinning hair, and wire-rimmed glasses. Like the other two people he had seen—how long had it been?—the man wore white.

"Captain Frost," the man began pleasantly, the English perfect-sounding but accented.

"Dr. Livingston, I presume?" Frost asked.

"Ah—your sense of humor. You have not lost it. For you, that is a pity," he smiled. Then, looking past Frost, he said something in Russian and the nurse pushed Frost down into a chair opposite the desk—it was wooden, hard, but comfortable feeling. There were no electrodes. More was said in Russian and Frost could hear the sound of the woman's rubber-soled shoes on the floor, then the door opening and closing shut. "Now—we are alone. Relax."

Frost smiled, then cocked his head down toward the straitjacket. "Not easy to do."

"Ah—but the straitjacket? That is what you call it in English? The straitjacket is necessary."

"Am I dangerous?"

"Igor would say that."

"Igor?" and Frost laughed in spite of himself. "The big guy?"

"Yes—Igor is large. But you are whom I wish to discuss, Captain Frost."

"Is this Russia?"

"Yes. Moscow to be precise."

"How long have I been a prisoner?"

"We prefer the word patient—two weeks exactly. You have been through the tests nine times. You have failed miserably all nine times. That is your misfortune."

"I don't follow you," Frost said.

"Your resentment, your determination—it has been

impossible to get an accurate brain wave scan. I am afraid you have left us with little choice. It is either euthanasia or permanent institutionalization. I will do what I can for you. I admire your courage."

Frost swallowed hard, unable to say anything for the moment, then, "Insti—"

"Institutionalization—yes," the man nodded.

"For what? Why am I here?"

The doctor stood up, taking a hypodermic needle from a black leatherette syringe case on his desk. "This is a mild sedative, very mild, but it should allow you a decent sleep. It won't put you out. I will know your fate tomorrow morning at dawn."

"I hate getting up that early," Frost smiled.

"You laugh in the face of death—or worse, perhaps. I admire you sincerely," the doctor smiled. He stopped beside Frost in the chair. "It is only a sedative—will I need assistance in administering it?"

The one-eyed man realized this was a step—a man in whom Frost could place his trust, his confidence. Then gradually—whatever it was they wanted—Frost would give the man, as a friend, as a confidant. The one-eyed man knew the drill. And he could take advantage of it more by not fighting it. "Go ahead. I don't have much choice."

"Thank you," the man smiled genuinely. "I'll get two of the security guards to assist you to your room. I don't trust Igor to be alone with you."

"Thank you," Frost nodded. As the needle went in, Frost wondered what exactly they wanted him to confess to.

He was already starting to feel relaxed, almost mellow, as two men in Soviet army uniforms walked in, AKM assault rifles slung on their shoulders.

Chapter Four

Frost opened his eye. The room was the same—he had memorized the spots on the ceiling where it had been carelessly painted. He could move his hands, his legs, and a white blanket was covering him. He sat up, the medicine cabinet gone. The restraint straps were missing from their stirrup-shaped receptacles.

He rubbed his eye, trying to think. He had had a good sleep, albeit his mouth tasted odd. He wondered when he'd brushed his teeth last. It felt like weeks ago from the film he could feel with his tongue.

"Two weeks," he murmured. And he wondered: It could have been three weeks, or three days—all the more to disorient him, to make him cling to the doctor. He was the man they would want him to identify with, gradually see as a friend, a father-figure, someone to please.

Frost leaned back, then lay down on the bed. That he was even in Russia he doubted. He remembered an ambulance, and what seemed like an airplane ride. He remembered seeing light through gauze, like the way he had been able to see faint traces of light with his right eye when the surgery had been done on his left. He remembered Russian-sounding voices. Perhaps he was in Russia after all. He tried to think why.

Was it the conflict with the KGB he had been involved in some time back—with Doctor Kulley and the Satanists?* But the KGB wasn't in the revenge business usually, and if they had been, it would have been a simple hit, not a kidnap or brain washing, this whole thing he had undergone. This was some operation, and there was something they wanted, something—

There was a loud knock at the door, then the sound of a lock being undone, and the door opened. A helmeted, uniformed Soviet soldier stepped inside, AKM slung on his shoulder. He gestured and Frost stood up.

"Wait," Frost murmured.

The man looked quizzical, jerking his right thumb toward the door. Frost pointed down toward his own crotch and made a hissing sound, saying, "Tinkle—you know," and he smiled.

He walked into the open-doored bathroom and stood in front of the urinal. He could attempt to disarm the guard, but there was one standing outside the door as well.

It wasn't the time, but he didn't think there'd be much more time somehow. He did what he had to do and turned. The big female nurse was standing beside the guard, a straitjacket extended at the ends of her arms.

Frost sighed heavily, slipping his arms into it. He felt the sleeves secured behind him, felt a reasonable, gentle nudge from her and started walking. Straitjackets, he thought. He wished that when he was a boy he had read more about Houdini. . . .

Frost sat opposite the doctor—he remembered the face better now—had seen it before the previous interview, peering down at him, studying him.

*See *They Call Me the Mercenary #13: Naked Blade, Naked Gunn*

The face looked up now—there was no smile in the eyes.

"I am sorry, Captain Frost—I know you would have preferred death. But it is to be permanent institutionalization."

Frost watched the snow outside the window, happy he'd already urinated. . . .

Chapter Five

Frost was almost getting used to sitting with his arms permanently folded.

"What does permanent institutionalization mean, Doctor?" he said, making his voice calm. He wasn't calm. He was afraid. He should have made the play for the guard when he had the chance.

"You will be given a series of drugs. You wouldn't know their names anyway, I'm afraid. They will work on your brain to induce a permanent state of what you might best recognize as paranoid schizophrenia. You will be treated well, fed, cared for. It will not be a totally useless life. At times at least."

"Rubber room—and this?" and Frost moved his arms inside the straitjacket.

"This rubber room—a padded cell?"

"Yes," Frost intoned.

"Yes," the doctor answered.

"Why—tell me that?"

"I respect you—your courage. Yes, I will tell you why," the man nodded, sitting down again behind his desk. Frost watched the snow as he listened. "For several years now," the man began. "Soviet science and medicine has worked together to obviate the awkward problem of liquidating, institutionalizing, or imprisoning political dissidents, Captain. What you in the West would call brain cleaning."

"Brain washing," Frost corrected automatically in his forced calm.

"Brain washing, yes. What you would call brain washing we have always found to leave something to be desired—a lack of permanence, the odd ways in which preprogrammed responses must be elicited, et cetera. And it has been possible for persons such as yourself to resist for any extended period of time, so the previous methods were often times not cost effective—"

"Inflation's tough on everybody," Frost smiled.

"Quite—very perceptive of you. In a regulated economy such as ours, there too are financial pressures to be dealt with. And then," the doctor continued, smiling, "there has always been the time factor. Brain clean—er, washing—it even with a receptive subject takes time. Sometimes there is woefully little."

"In recent years of course," he went on, "institutionalizing dissidents in mental hospitals has become more widely accepted. You will go to such a place yourself soon." He glanced at Frost, the smile almost sheepish-looking, embarrassed, Frost thought. The one-eyed man decided they didn't want him to confess to anything. He was part of something which evidently hadn't worked and was now being disposed of. He looked at the doctor in a new light. The man really was sincere, wasn't just trying to get his confidence. Frost felt terrified at this. He had read about Soviet mental hospitals, heard about Soviet psychiatrists' procedures being condemned by their international colleagues. Death was the better option.

"At any event," the doctor went on, "a new and very promising procedure has been developed." His eyes twinkled with evident pride. "A direct result of Soviet leadership in space technology actually. Electrodes—very sophisticated. One must be a scientist of the highest order to really understand their workings. Not like the things attached to your body when we searched for a brain scan. Very modern, sophisticated. We have found these can be implanted successfully in the living tissue of the human brain. They can be coordinated by low-frequency laser pulse—a way both you Americans and the Soviets use even now to communicate with submarines. And this is vastly more easily done through the use of satellite relays. We can implant the electrode here, and control someone—well," and he smiled again, gesturing out his snow-packed window. "We can control someone way over there—perhaps in the United States or China. The possibilities are virtually limitless.

"Now," he continued enthusiastically, "the political dissident can be made completely politically acceptable, simply by a constant pulse being sent to him through the electrode. Everyone is happier—even the subject. Just prior to the recent changes in the KGB, it was proposed that select native Americans could be so programmed for use at some politically or strategically decisive moment in the distant future."

"Unconscious agents," Frost interrupted.

"Quite. You were to be an experiment. Unfortunately for you—" The doctor didn't finish the sentence.

"Gee," Frost smiled.

"It was impossible, I'm afraid, to get an accurate brain scan. Which is needed of course to calibrate the electrode implantation, and—sadly—cannot be gotten while a subject is under the influence of drugs."

"Can't have everything," Frost smiled, his eyes scanning the room for a letter opener, anything. But in the straitjacket—how could he fight, even if a weapon were available.

"And so, I'm afraid there's nothing more to do for

you. We've so far had great success. There was a ballerina, for example, continuously trying to defect. But so beautiful," the doctor said, almost lovingly. "We implanted an electrode; she is now a model Soviet citizen. And, should we ever require her services in some other way, perhaps when she is performing before some diplomatic body, or the U.N.—something like that. I of course abhor violence, but the needs of the state take precedence over the individual."

"No shit," Frost nodded. There was nothing even remotely like a weapon in the room.

"Is there any, I believe the phrase is 'last request', you might have, Captain Frost?"

"I don't suppose a set of clothes, an assault rifle and an hour's head start would—"

The doctor laughed. "The sense of humor—it is in your file. I noticed a photograph in your wallet of a blonde-haired woman. I presume that to be the Jewish journalist, Bess Stallman?"

"Last request, yeah. Throw the photo away and don't use it."

"A fair request—it can be lost," the man nodded.

Frost decided the doctor, in his own perverse way, wasn't really such a bad guy—just a psycho.

Chapter Six

Frost stood in the hallway, cold in his hospital gown and straitjacket, but cold for other reasons beside the temperature of the hallway. The two guards and the nurse stood around him. Behind him, the doctor stood in the doorway of his office.

"A bit of advice, Captain Frost? Professional?"

"Yes," Frost said absently, trying to think—two guards, two AKMs—a chance at death at least. But a fast run would net him nothing but a disabling injection. "Yes," and Frost looked at the man, for the first time noticing the doctor was slightly taller than himself. "What, Doctor?"

"Do not attempt to fight the injections. The faster they take hold the easier it will be for you. All your subconscious fantasies—you will live in them. Good and bad. I hope for you they are good."

The one-eyed man licked his lips. "You said a last request—well I've got another one. And it just might make me able to live in the good ones. Please," Frost implored. "Her picture—let me see it, touch it? One more time?"

"The woman?"

"Yes—Bess. Please, Doctor."

The doctor glanced at his watch. Quitting time? Frost wondered.

"Yes, of course," then he said something in Russian and the two guards and the nurse stepped back. Then the doctor paused, and said in English, "I have read your file. Hairbreadth escapes seem to be your stock in trade, cheating fate. You will see the picture—but so will they." He summoned the guards in Russian.

The doctor started back into his office, the two guards and the woman around him. He didn't look back, but heard the office door close.

Frost approached the desk, standing in front of it, watching as the doctor unlocked a file cabinet, extracting an expandable file, pulling out a manila file inside of it, then inverting the larger, expandable file on the desktop. Frost watched, seeing it almost in slow motion. His Rolex, the one Bess made him buy. His money clip, the money still in it. The keys to his apartment, the one he shared with Bess. The keys to the '78 LTD he'd bought for the move south, the best used car he'd ever owned. He saw his wallet, light brown, bulging with credit cards and I.D.

The doctor opened the wallet, shuffling the almost brand-new Georgia driver's license, the concealed weapons permit, the motor club card—all of it onto the desk. And laminated in plastic, the picture of Bess.

"It is here," the doctor said, setting it before him. "I'm sorry, my friend."

Frost nodded, feeling inside that he wanted to cry. He would never see the face again, except perhaps in a nightmare, the blonde hair, the green eyes.

"Can I touch it—please?" Frost asked.

"Ah—"

"Look—there're four of you—they've got guns. What am I gonna do—please?"

In Russian then, the doctor barked a command. Frost

felt the hands behind him, heard the slap of the nurse's shoes against the floor. His arms were free. He could barely move them. He felt the buckles at the back of the straitjacket being opened.

The doctor himself helped Frost remove the straitjacket.

"Your picture," the doctor said noncommittally.

Frost took a step closer to the desk, rubbing his arms with his hands to get out the stiffness. He picked up the watch then. It was running, but he had no idea of the accuracy of the time or date—he doubted both. He fingered the keys, holding them as he picked up Bess's picture. He loved her. He felt he'd never realized that more than at this instant. Death was something that went with the rules—this wasn't.

"Fate worse than death," Frost said under his breath.

"What?" the Russian doctor asked.

Frost reached to the desk top, dropping Bess's picture, the glass desk cover in his hands.

The nurse started to scream. Frost smashed the glass—a quarter inch thick or better—across the face of the nearest AKM-armed Soviet soldier, his left foot snapping up and out into the crotch of the second guard.

The one-eyed man wheeled, his right fist loose of the glass now hammering into the doctor's jaw, punching the man back into the desk and over it.

The nurse was reaching for him. Frost backstepped, her hands coming for his throat, his tired arms raising up, hammering against the insides of her elbows. He broke her grip as it started. Then, his left hauling back, a short jab snapping forward, he caught her at the tip of her jaw, driving her back.

Frost wheeled again, the second guard recovering, the first guard dead in a pool of blood on the floor.

Frost's right snapped out—too slowly. The guard's

AKM came up into a guard position, blocking Frost's punch, the rifle swinging down, the muzzle aimed at Frost's skull.

Frost sidestepped, snapping a short kick into the man's knee caps with his left foot. Then he hammered out with his left fist, the keys in the fist still like a knuckle duster. The fist connected. Frost winced, almost screaming with the pain—the fingers might have been broken, he realized.

He felt something hammer at his back, drive him forward, his crotch smashing against the edge of the desk.

He rolled, away from whatever it was, falling off the desk, to the floor.

It was the nurse. She was saying something in Russian. He figured it wasn't anything he'd want to repeat.

Frost feigned a swing with his right, the woman ducking professionally. But Frost pulled back, half wheeling left, his right foot snapping up, going for her face. The heel of his bare foot hit the right side of her head in a fast double kick. The one-eyed man lost his balance, falling. The woman sprawled back. Then she pushed herself up, coming at him in a low run, hands extended.

Frost sidestepped right, jumping a jagged piece of glass with his bare feet. He jumped again, wheeling, his right foot snapping out, crossing over her as she ducked. The one-eyed man shifted his balance onto his right foot, jumping to twist himself around, then he lashed out in a high, flying kick, his left foot crashing into the woman's face. He could feel, hear, almost taste the crunch of bone as the nose broke and rammed upward into the brain.

Blood spurted from her face. The eyes glassy, her body toppled toward him as he recovered. He caught the body and shoved back, the dead woman dropping like a sawed tree.

Frost glanced at her once, murmuring, "I hope there aren't any more at home like you, honey."

He bent to the glass strewn floor, noticing his left foot was bleeding. Frost picked up the AKM, checking the chamber, leaving the safety off, then snapped the butt upward at the second trooper starting feebly from the floor. "Eat it," Frost remarked.

The doctor was stirring. Frost started toward him.

"No—please," the man implored.

"Call us even," Frost rasped, smiling. His left fist jabbed out, crossing the doctor's jaw, slamming the body back against the wall. The doctor slumped down beside the window.

Frost picked up Bess's picture. He felt foolish, but he kissed it.

Chapter Seven

If he remembered Soviet rank properly, the man was a corporal, Frost decided. It was a big comedown from a captaincy.

His clothes had not been in the doctor's office. "Kiss off another pair of sixty-five dollar shoes," he'd rasped.

He studied himself briefly in the mirror. No eye patch, no sunglasses—just one rather average good eye and one rather unpleasant-looking scar. He pulled the helmet down lower and crinkled up the left side of his face. It hid the eye scar a little.

He had set the Rolex from the cheap Russian timepiece the doctor had worn, but Frost had not put the watch back on his wrist. An expensive watch would have been a dead giveaway. He would have enough trouble, speaking no Russian and hiding the scar where his left eye should have been. His weapons were gone—the little Gerber knife and the Metalifed Browning High Power. Neither of the Soviet guards had carried a pistol, but aside from selecting the best of the two AKMs the guards had carried, he had taken the spare magazines for both assault rifles; now he had five spares plus one in the gun. He doubted it would be enough to get him out of Russia.

The one-eyed man looked at Bess's picture once more, then returned it to his wallet with his other things. He pocketed the car keys as well. He didn't imagine ever being able to use them again, but they could make a weapon if needed as they had before.

The doctor was stirring on the floor, the relaxed sphincter muscle of one of the dead guards having made the office smell badly. The doctor was coughing. Frost hated to, but he slapped the man to momentary consciousness and socked him on the jaw again, putting him out.

He had only the doctor's word that he was actually in Moscow—and if he were there was one, slim chance. He quickly searched the doctor's desk, finding a telephone book. If he remembered the cyrillic lettering correctly, it read in part, "Moscow." He had the papers of the guard whose uniform he had taken—but the face looked nothing like his own and he didn't know the right Russian words if someone asked for papers anyway.

Frost walked across the room, putting his hand on the doorknob. "Oh, boy," he murmured. He didn't have enough fingers to cross, he realized. He opened the door and stepped into the hallway.

He stepped back inside. He wondered. He walked back to the doctor's desk and picked up the telephone book. There was a map, in the front portion, of central Moscow. He realized even if it were printed plainly, he couldn't read it—the American Embassy. Where? "Shit," he murmured, then he dropped the telephone book.

He walked back to the doorway, opened it and again stepped into the hallway, nodding to the unconscious and dead people inside, then closing the door and starting briskly down the hallway—away from the direction of the room with the chair.

The one-eyed man reached the end of the corridor

and stopped. It formed a "T." He started off to his right, for all he knew heading deeper into the building.

He stopped before two wide swinging doors. There was lettering on them and above them was a sign.

Frost checked the safety of the AKM. It would have to be set to on or otherwise attract a suspicious eye. But his thumb was near it. He stepped through the doors. A woman, smoothing down her skirt as she stood up from a doorless stalled toilet stared at him, her mouth wide open. Frost smiled and gave her a little salute, then stepped back outside. He glanced at the sign again—at least he'd remember the letters for "Ladies" next time.

He glanced up and down the corridor—then started walking again.

At the far end of the corridor, past many white-painted doors, he saw a glass door and beyond it a guard. He assumed it was the way out—he'd given up on reading signs.

He walked confidently toward the glass door and opened it. The guard there relaxed; he turned to Frost, smiling. The smile faded and Frost snapped the butt of his AKM up into the base of the man's jaw, the head snapping back. The guard slumped back against the wall beside what, in America, Frost would have called a Thompson chair—the school desk-chair combination one saw so often in high schools and colleges. Frost guessed it might have been sent to Russia on Lend Lease during World War II.

The guard had something Frost dearly wanted—a pistol. The one-eyed man reached to the guard's belt and opened the flap holster there. The pistol was a Makarov, 9x18 mm caliber, a weak-sistered version of the 9mm Parabellum, like Frost used in his High Power. With the Soviet propensity for inversion—morality and everything else, he mused—the safety worked in the opposite manner of most pistols, moving the slide-mounted safety down put the pistol into the firing mode. He worked the base of the butt magazine catch, checking the in-line type box magazine—a full eight rounds were visible through the skeletonized sides. The chamber was empty. Frost reinserted the magazine, jacked the slide back and let it slam forward. He left the safety off, then manually lowered the hammer. A double action, he knew the trigger pull would be long enough without worrying over a safety. He stuffed the pistol under his uniform tunic, then quickly searched the man for anything else useful. There was a Hershey bar—how the man had gotten it, Frost didn't know. The chocolate was discolored and old seeming, so Frost left it. There were two spare magazines for the pistol, and Frost took these. There was also a knife, what looked like a Japanese-made push button. Frost worked the button, the knife flicking open with an unreassuring tinny sound. He closed the knife and pocketed it.

The one-eyed man looked beyond the glass door. There were double-wide wooden doors, leading, he hoped, to the street.

Beside the guard were two buzzers, one red and one green. Electric wires ran around the top of the door-frame and Frost assumed the locking mechanism of the doors was controlled by one of the buttons, the other the alarm.

He placed his index finger over the green button—it should be for the doors, he assumed. "Should be," the one-eyed man smiled. He remembered the safety of the Makarov. Backwards. He pushed the red button, there was a gentle buzzing sound and the door made a clicking sound. When he removed his finger from the button, the door clicked again.

"Hmm," Frost murmured. He bent low over the unconscious soldier, hefting the man and pulling him up into his arms. The two buttons were six inches apart.

Frost needed a weight, though. He lowered the unconscious guard slowly over the red button, the body weighting it down, the buzzing sound beginning. The door latch clicked and Frost walked quickly toward it, opening it.

He glanced behind him once.

"Shit," he murmured, the body slumping, the man starting to awaken. The green buzzer was smothered under his weight—and an alarm bell began to ring.

The one-eyed man stepped through the doors and into a snow-covered street and beyond it what would in summer have been perhaps a green area, and now, ice-coated, what seemed to be hundreds of children of ages varying from toddler to teen, played hockey.

A massive gray building was to his right—and—from an article or a film—Frost somehow recognized it. He knew the place he was at, the only place in Moscow he would have recognized. It was Dzerzhinsky Square. The gray building housed the headquarters of the KGB.

"Holy—" Frost saw the steam on his breath, heard the ringing of the alarm bell and started across the street, toward the children playing hockey. He dodged a streetcar and reached the border of the massive ice rink, street lights winking at him in yellow from across the street by the building he had just left. And in the old gray edifice opposite it, lights were coming on—more yellow lights. It would be the KGB, responding to the alarm at their "hospital" across the way. Frost turned, starting to walk, bordering the ice rink, children laughing, shouting, screaming with delight. An old woman was coming toward him. Frost smiled and nodded, sidestepping her. She grabbed his arm.

She was speaking to him in Russian, saying something fast and totally unintelligible and urgent sounding. She shook him, apparently because he didn't answer. Then she pointed—there was a young girl, lying on the edge of the ice, holding her leg, blood edging between her fingers.

Frost instantly knew what the woman wanted. In Russia a soldier and a policeman were sometimes interchangeable. As a soldier he would know something about first aid. A knot of young people was around her. Likely, other help had been summoned. If he walked away she would be suspicious, but if he stayed . . . he spoke no Russian. What would draw more attention? he asked himself. And then the one-eyed man looked at the Russian girl's face—it was pale, paler than any normal face should be, the hands clasping the right shin and knee covered with blood.

Frost nodded to the old woman, patting her forearm and walking past her, toward the little girl.

The one-eyed man tried to keep to character, shoving, not too rudely though, the knot of watchers aside. He dropped to his knees in the snow beside the girl.

She looked up at him, her face pretty despite its paleness. She was perhaps fourteen, if even that. She let loose a stream of words in a pretty-sounding alto. Frost couldn't understand even one of the words.

"Hmm," he murmured, assuming that to be a universal expression. He gently pried her bloody fingers away from her leg. The pants leg was soaked through and sticky. He reached into the pocket of his uniform tunic for the pushbutton knife, flicking the blade. There was a general expression of shock from the crowd. He didn't pay any attention to it.

Using the knife, as gently as he could, he cut up the seam of the pants leg, revealing a high woolen sock beneath it. It had been white, but was now red and soaked with the blood. He worked gently, but the girl winced, reaching out her right bloodied hand to hold his forearm.

Frost could say nothing, and trying to hide his absent

left eye he looked at her and smiled.

The girl's eyes looked pained—then shocked. She had seen the eye. But she smiled back.

Frost rolled down the stocking, the calf beneath it gushing blood. He assumed it had been a skate blade, perhaps the front tip hooking into her leg. In Viet Nam and since then in Latin America and Africa, he had seen enough bleeders. This was a bad one. In less than a few minutes, the girl would be unconscious; and minutes after that she could be dead.

"Aagh," he moaned, almost saying something in English.

He wanted to tell her something, to take the look of panic from her eyes as she stared at the wound. Gently, he reached out his left hand and touched her chin, then turned her face away—he always did that himself whenever he got a shot. He hated watching someone tinker with his injured body.

The one-eyed man assumed help was on the way, that proper medical attention would be given in minutes. For that reason, he decided on the only thing he could do to stop the bleeding—a tourniquet.

The girl had a scarf covering her hair—which looked to be silk. Gently, he reached toward her face and undid the knot under her chin, then slipped the scarf from her head. Her eyes were wide—puzzled, he guessed. He twisted the scarf into a rope, then gently began to bind it just under her knee. The snow-covered ground offered no sticks to use to twist the tourniquet for pressure. He closed the push-button knife, inserted it between the two parts of the knot and started to twist. Visibly, the bleeding from the four-inch-long gash began to ebb, then all but stopped.

There was a long sigh from someone in the crowd around him—a woman, he thought.

The little girl—he guessed she wasn't really that

little—seemed barely conscious now, but as he made to stand, she leaned up and kissed his cheek.

The one-eyed man wished he knew how to say in Russian, "Thank you." Instead, he smiled.

A man stood beside him, and Frost grabbed the man's right hand and almost forced the man into a crouch to hold the knife in place for the tourniquet pressure.

In the background, he could hear the sound of a siren—perhaps the ambulance for the girl. He caught sight of the old woman who'd originally summoned him to aid the girl. She was crossing herself, making the last portions of the sign from right to left as is the practice in Eastern churches.

The one-eyed man man nodded to her, starting into the knot of people. At its far edge were two men in Soviet uniform, and with them a third man, looking for all the world, Frost thought, like a refugee from a B-movie version of World War II. He wore a black leather trenchcoat and a dark brown fedora hat, the hat cocked back on his head, a gray woolen scarf around his neck.

"KGB," Frost muttered. And the man was staring at him. Frost's mind raced. If he started shooting, they'd start shooting. The crowd of bystanders behind him didn't matter, nor did the girl whose life he'd just saved.

He walked toward them, the KBG man still staring, reaching under his coat. Frost kept walking, the man's gloveless right hand producing a pistol. There was a shout in Russian, then repeated in English, "Halt!"

The one-eyed man made two fast steps out, swinging the rifle under his arm on its sling, grasping the small of the stock, snapping out the butt of the weapon into the KGB man's face. The KGB man stumbled backwards into the two uniformed men flanking him.

Frost started to run across the ice, his feet slipping, going down to his knees.

He rolled, scrambled up to his feet, slipping again, heaving toward a smallish woman with a hockey stick. They spilled to the ground, Frost's rifle skittering across the ice.

"Shit," the one-eyed man rasped.

He rolled, snatching up the hockey stick as the nearest of the two Soviet soldiers lunged for him. Frost rammed the hockey stick up and outward, the blade at the base of the stick punching into the soldier's crotch. There was a scream. Frost got to his feet, his right foot snapping out as the soldier doubled forward. Frost's heel connected with the soldier's jawline. The head snapped back with an audible cracking sound, the neck breaking, Frost guessed.

Frost snatched up the man's rifle, the sounds of whistles in the distance behind him now, blowing like insane teakettles, incessantly.

The KGB man and the second soldier were running toward him across the ice.

Frost found the AKM's safety, working it, hoping the chamber was loaded, leveling it. He had a clear field if he controlled his bursts. He pumped the trigger, the thirty-caliber assault rifle humping in his hands. The soldier spun out, going down; the KGB man dropped to the ice, firing his pistol. Frost let loose another burst and caught the man in the neck and face, then turned and slipped on the ice. But he caught himself and kept running—hard.

The street was perhaps fifty yards distant when he hit the snow. Then he was running faster, easier now, his breath coming in short gasps of steam, his muscles and lungs aching.

He vaulted a snowbank, skidding on the ice on the opposite side, falling to his knees, pushing himself up. Hands reached out to him, grabbing at him. Frost caught sight of the face—just an ordinary Russian being a good citizen and stopping a man fleeing from the law. Frost punched him, then continued running.

To his far right now, opposite the next street, he could see a Roman-looking building—a museum or a theater, he supposed. He kept running, a streetcar homing in toward him as he crossed the street. The one-eyed man jumped for it, catching onto an ice-encrusted handrail, his hands slipping.

He leaned forward, hugging his body to it, catching his breath. The vehicle passed what looked like another museum and beyond it the street broadened drastically. Behind him, Frost heard the wailing of sirens.

He jumped for it.

Frost looked to right and left, not knowing Moscow but seeing large public buildings ahead of him. He started running, toward them. Soldiers or KGB would be less likely to shoot a hole in a public building than a private one, he guessed.

He looked to his left as he ran down the center of the street, dodging trucks and a few private cars, slipping, sliding on the new snowfall. He thought he was crazy—a department store?

He looked to his right. "Holy shit," he murmured. He'd seen it in a dozen May Day parade newsreels—Lenin's Tomb. "Hi, Nicolai!" Frost shouted at the top of his lungs, running.

A siren was growing louder behind him and he wheeled, wrenching the AKM off his shoulder.

A police car, he guessed. A man leaned out the passenger window, a gun in his hand. Frost let fire with the AKM, emptying the magazine into the driver's side window as he dodged to his right. The car spun out, smashing into a large gate on the right hand side of the end of the street.

Frost started running after it, the man from the passenger side crawling out of the vehicle, raising the pistol. Frost shouldered the AKM, a fresh magazine inserted into it as soon as he'd fired it out, then pressed the trigger. A burst from the AKM sliced across the roof of the car and into the man, the body slumping down and out of sight.

Frost reached the car, the engine still running, the windshield gone, a dead man slumped behind the wheel. Frost rolled the body out into the snow, then slid behind the wheel, the AKM on the seat beside him.

Manual transmission—he hunted for reverse, found it and with a grating sound, the car started back, away from the gate.

Frost stomped the brakes. More sirens could be heard behind him now, men running into the street, some of them in uniform. He wrenched the stick, not finding first, but finding second. He gave the car gas, popping the clutch. The automobile lumbered forward. He cut the wheel hard right as suddenly the compression caught up, the car lurching ahead. The left front fender, already wrinkled and dented, slammed into the side of a truck, part of the fender peeling away. Frost cut the wheel hard right around the gate, then stomped the clutch, upshifting, the speedometer needle bouncing up.

There was a cathedral far over on his right. Ahead of him was a street and just beyond it a bridge. He stomped the clutch and upshifted once more, hammering down three soldiers running at him. He stomped the gas, popping the clutch, the car shooting ahead.

Two men were coming up on his left. Frost reached under his tunic, snatching at the pistol there, finding it. Punching the pistol out the window, he fired twice, nailing one of the men, the second man dropping back.

Snow and bits of glass sprayed at his face as he drove, the car's slipstream racing through the shot-out windshield ahead of him.

At the center of the bridge was a car, shifting into

position to block the bridge.

Frost pressed his foot all the way down to the floor, bracing himself, the left front fender impacting into the rear end of the black sedan. Both cars locked for an instant, then Frost's car broke away. A man jumped from the car—Frost could see him in the sideview mirror. Then the man was gone and so was the car, engulfed in a black and orange ball of flame. The gas tank had exploded.

Frost's ears rang with it.

At the end of the bridge he cut a sharp right, not knowing where he was going but avoiding two police cars converging on the corner from in front of him and to his left.

He saw a flag to his left, toward the middle of the block. It was the British Union Jack.

"Yahoo!" the one-eyed man heard himself scream.

Police cars were behind him, more coming up in front of him. And overhead, he thought he heard the droning of a helicopter.

There was nothing else for it.

Frost cut the wheel sharply left, toward the wrought-iron gates of the embassy, up the small drive. His right hand wrenched up the emergency brake, his foot hammering down on the brake and the clutch. He slammed the stick into neutral. Running toward the gates, the police sirens were behind him. Then gunfire—he could hear it, almost feel it.

"Halt!"

Frost wheeled, a police car bearing down on him, to crush him against the gates.

The one-eyed man jumped, reaching up. Finding a finial, he hauled himself up, his left trouser leg catching on the top of the gates.

Men were below him, men in British uniforms.

"American—American!" Frost shouted, rolling off

the top of the gate, falling. The concrete slammed up toward him, his left arm aching like a rotten tooth, his head hurting.

"All right, mate!" Frost heard the voice and looked up. He never thought he'd feel like kissing a man with a walrus mustache.

Chapter Eight

"Well, you've had quite the grand tour, Captain Frost. Let's see," the slim white-haired man began, sifting through a sheaf of papers. "You escaped from the Dzerzhinsky Institute For Psychiatric Research—"

Frost laughed.

The man behind the desk looked up, then back to his paperwork, continuing, "Then illegally boarded a public transport somewhere near the Bolshoi Ballet Theater—that Greco-Roman building you described. You were in a running gun battle on the street between Lenin's Tomb and the GUM Department Store, then caused a state-owned vehicle to crash—" he consulted his notes in greater detail apparently. "Yes, near the Spassky Gate. I'm surprised you didn't drive it into St. Basil's Cathedral after you commandeered the car—the cathedral was so terribly close. Then, you took the subject vehicle across the Moscow River, then invaded British territory—here."

"Did I do all that?" Frost smiled.

"Yes—you did all that."

"What kind of car was it I stole?" Frost asked after a moment.

"A Zil actually, not a bad motorcar as the Russian ones go."

"I like a Ford better—maybe a Pontiac."

"I'll note that in my summary," the white-haired man smiled. "I've received—or I should say, Sir Arthur, the ambassador, has received a personal memorandum from Mr. Andropov—"

"*The* Mr. Andropov?"

"Yes, Yuri Andropov, the gentleman who replaced the late Mr. Brezhnev. All the memorandum alluded to was a speedy resolution of this crisis. I so terribly wish you had driven on. You could have simply followed the Moscow River out to the Garden Ring, turned right and driven along a bit and you would have seen your own embassy. It's right there on the left, hard to miss."

"Didn't have a map," Frost smiled.

"Quite," the older man nodded.

"Are you guys gonna throw me out?"

The older man smiled. "Hardly, dear boy. We've verified as much of your tale of woe as possible. If we return you, the Russian chaps are going to think they can kidnap a British subject off British soil next. No, we shan't return you, but I'm afraid you're destined to be a rather permanent guest here, at least for the foreseeable future. They cannot come in, but you cannot go out, of course. It appears they wish to discuss with you the murder of two guards and a nurse at the hospital, and the deaths of several other persons along the way here."

The older man then removed his silver wire-rimmed glasses, smiling. "But our own sources also indicate that you saved the life of a young girl who was bleeding to death in an ice field opposite the hospital."

"Well—I don't know if I saved her life or not, Mr. Heath, but—"

"I doubt you'd spurn credit for the killing of the guards in order to manage your escape. So please, don't spurn credit for such a selfless deed." Heath put his glasses back on. "I don't mean to sound unpleasant when I say it would have better for all concerned had you gone to the American Embassy. In fact, in all candor, I'm honored—and I'm sure Her Majesty's Government is as well—that you placed such faith in us. I'm sure it was more like the Americanism, 'any port in a storm', as it were, but while you are here you'll be given the same courtesies and protection that would be afforded to a British subject. I'm afraid, however, Captain Frost, that you'll have to be a bit careful walking in our garden. The wall, as you well know, isn't difficult to scale." Heath laughed for a moment. "I say—this is the most excitement we've had here in quite some time."

"Anything to help," Frost nodded. He had decided to try to quit smoking. Instead now, he found his battered Zippo, one of the other items he'd rescued from the doctor's office, and took one of the Players from the box in the pocket of his borrowed British Army khaki shirt. He lit it in the blue-yellow flame of the lighter. "Has my Embassy been notified?"

"Most certainly, dear boy. The very first thing, of course. This evening at dinner, one of your chaps will come round and discuss the American point of view. I've arranged for some suitable clothes to be found for you by then. But the Americans can do little for you. They will find themselves just as unable to get you out of Russia as are we, I'm afraid."

"That's why I haven't told you everything, Mr. Heath."

"You've alluded to that before, Captain—what is this strange story?"

Frost interrupted. "The Russians were planning to drug me into a state of permanent mental illness."

"So you've said," Heath nodded soberly.

"Since they figured I'd never be in a position to bother them, they told me something, something my government and your government would be dying to know about, something involving the national security of all the Western Nations."

"What is it?"

Frost smiled, dragging heavily on the cigarette. "That's exactly what I won't talk about—not while I'm in Russia." Frost studied his hands, then looked up into Heath's watery blue eyes. The man had his glasses off, as if studying Frost. "And if it isn't too much bother, could you call that U.S. Embassy guy—maybe see if he's got a few 'gift' cartons of Camels lying around?" Players were a good cigarette, but he liked his own better. The embassy had provided him a comfortable room as well, with a comfortable bed—but he liked his own better, and the company of the woman who shared it. "Ask him, won't you?" Frost added.

Chapter Nine

Frost studied himself in the mirror—a new eyepatch, a new pair of slacks from the GUM Department Store and a fresh pair of sixty-five-dollar shoes. An Embassy secretary had taken his size and picked up a supply of clothes for him that afternoon. He had never owned a pink shirt before, but women tended to pick bizarre colors in men's clothing. He shrugged, taking the woolen sweater and pulling it on. It was one of those like the British commandoes always wore in the World War II movies—a gun patch at the right shoulder and elbow patches, these of suede. He glanced at the black luminous face of the Rolex Oyster Perpetual Sea Dweller on his left wrist. It was hard for him to realize that about twenty-four hours earlier he had been escaping from a mental hospital; and almost twenty-four hours ago precisely he had stormed his way into the British Embassy.

He had seen to it that, although personal contact by telephone was out, a message had been gotten out to Bess in the British diplomatic pouch, to let her know he was alive and well.

He took his things—the wallet, money clip and lighter and keys—and started toward the door. He stopped, glancing at himself once more in the mirror. With the very British sweater, and his eyepatch restored, he decided there might be a future for him in shirt advertisements. He shrugged, hit the light switch and walked out. . .

The presence of the dark-haired woman at the far end of Ambassador Sir Arthur Borne's table had never been explained, and as Frost sipped at his coffee, he watched her. She apparently wasn't watching him. She had come with the assistant to the American Charge d'Affaires and another man from the Embassy. Frost recognized the manner if not the face of this second man. The man was CIA, though likely posing as an assistant in a trade delegation. However, his real job function, at least to Frost, was unmistakable.

Throughout the long and deliciously ample dinner, there had been little else but small talk about the Soviet economy, the severity of the current winter—everything but Frost himself and his predicament.

"Mr. Heath," Sir Arthur finally said, "I suggest that you might prefer to continue the conversation with our American friends in the library. Perhaps Adolphe might bring you some brandy." Sir Arthur stood, and his guests followed his lead. "Affairs of state, gentlemen," Sir Arthur smiled good naturedly. He was a massive man, more what one pictured Robin Hood's Friar Tuck to have looked like than the common conception of a British diplomat.

"A splendid suggestion, Sir Arthur," Heath smiled. Then turning to Frost and the others, he said, "Gentlemen." And then speaking to the dark-haired woman, "And Miss Gorki?"

Frost nodded, studying the woman again briefly. Her hair was almost unbelievably dark, but the eyes still darker, the cheekbones high, like one expected in a model's face. "I'd find that most enjoyable, Mr. Heath," the woman answered, smiling at Heath and, in the brief instant, her eyes meeting Frost's. The one-eyed man could feel her gaze locked with his for an instant; and then the woman turned and walked toward the library on Heath's arm.

Frost shrugged, pushing back his chair and following, fishing in his pockets for a cigarette—Heath's secretary had brought three cartons of Camels with her from the department store. Frost was already working on the second pack. He lit a cigarette then as he walked into the library on the heels of the man he'd pegged as CIA.

Heath gestured toward a chair near the fireplace and Frost nodded, taking it, smelling the logs as they burned, hearing them crackle. Adolphe, the butler, arrived and Heath said, "A brandy, Adolphe—Captain?"

"The same," Frost nodded. Only the woman had a different after-dinner drink—Creme de Menthe. The CIA man asked for another cup of coffee.

Nothing was said, then Adolphe reappeared quickly, carrying a small silver tray and small glasses, serving Miss Gorki first, then Mr. Heath, then Frost and the other two men.

"A toast, gentlemen," Heath smiled, raising his tiny glass as Adolphe left the room. "To resolving the current crisis to the mutual satisfaction of all."

"A diplomat's toast if ever there was one," Frost smiled, nodding, sipping then at the brandy.

"I'm afraid, Captain," Heath smiled after a moment, "that a diplomat makes toasts like a diplomat because diplomats are the only persons who ever make toasts anymore." And he laughed.

"Five bucks if you can repeat that," Frost smiled.

"Now what the hell is goin' on here, Frost?"

"Ah—the CIA speaks," Frost nodded, glancing at the thin, dour-faced man.

"What's this national security shit—?"

"I say, Mr. Crane," Heath began. "A lady is present!"

"She works for us."

"Crane, he's right," the assistant Charge d'Affaires nodded, looking inadequate to Crane or anyone in the room.

"Fine," Crane nodded. "Let's all swap dumb-ass pleasantries for a while then." Crane returned to his coffee.

"I'll tell you what's up," Frost smiled, sipping again at his drink—he was beginning to relax. "In simple language, the KGB has a plot they're working right now, something important, something they were trying to brain wash me into getting involved with. I can give you all the poop so you can stop it."

"In exchange for what?" Crane rasped.

"For a ticket home—that's all," Frost felt himself smile, his voice low.

"Aww, sure—look, I'll give you a ticket. But you'll never be able to use it. You killed a bunch of their guys, made 'em all look like a bunch of ass—"

"Mr. Crane!" Heath cautioned.

"The point is," Frost interjected, "I don't want to spend the rest of my life here, and if you want to know what I know, you'll figure a way for me to get out. An escape route."

"Escape—from the middle of the Soviet Union?" Crane snapped.

"Escape from Russia. My word, that *would* upset them though," Heath laughed.

Frost was beginning to like Heath.

"That would be impossible," Miss Gorki added, her voice low, even, beautiful sounding. Her speech was very slightly accented. Russian?

Frost leaned back, downing the contents of his glass, setting the glass on a small octagon-shaped end table beside his chair. He lit another cigarette. "Impossible maybe. The only way you get the information you want, definitely."

"It would have to appear as though Captain Frost had engineered his own escape, as though he left our Embassy grounds without our knowledge, gentlemen," Heath added lamely.

"That's out of the question," the assistant Charge d'Affaires interjected.

Frost smiled, saying, "Like the guys in the laundries say, Crane—no tickie no washie." The one-eyed man closed his eye and listened to Crane breathing heavily. He would have rather listened to something else.

"Why do I have to learn Russian?" Frost asked Heath.

"I think our American friends feel that in the event they can somehow expedite your release without the knowledge of our Soviet friends, a working knowledge of the language might be of some use to you."

Frost laughed, looking at Heath sitting across the desk in the office and saying, "Seems to me that if the KGB kidnapped an American off American soil and the American made it to a Western Embassy, maybe the President or somebody could just get on the phone, tell the Commies to hang back or get their butts kicked and order somebody to drive me out to the nearest airfield."

"Ah—the outlook of the man not involved in the diplomatic process," and Heath took off his glasses and smiled. "I'd rather like it that way myself, actually. But I'm afraid the simple and direct approach is rarely tried these days. And usually when it is—"

"Yeah," Frost nodded. Resigning himself, Frost asked, "Okay, so when do I meet him?"

"Meet whom?"

"The Russian teacher."

"You've already met your instructor—or I should say, instructress—Miss Gorki." Heath kept smiling.

"*Skobleah eeta stoheat,*" Frost repeated, then looked

up into Miss Gorki's black eyes. "How much is this? What—you plannin' on getting me out of here through a restaurant or a whorehouse?"

"Captain Frost!"

"Just wanted to get your attention," Frost smiled.

"Let's try again, shall we," she smiled. "Now—we've just met, and of course, the logical question for me to ask, or for you to ask would be, *Kahc vah-shay eemyah.*"

"I'd say that when I met you—and it's a question?"

"Yes."

"I know," Frost smiled, raising his hand like a child might do in class.

"What is it then," she smiled.

"Does everyone tell you you're exquisite?"

"What?"

"Isn't that what I'd say?" Frost asked.

"No—no. It's, ah—What is your name? that's the question." She looked down to her books.

"Hank—"

"What?" and she looked up.

"You asked me my name—it's Hank," he told her, lighting a cigarette.

"Mine is Arika," she said, her voice soft. "You think I am—"

"Exquisite." Frost said. "Yes—that should be obvious to you every time you look in the mirror."

"I—" and she looked down at her books again, her eyelids closing for a brief instant, then looked back at him. "You will never learn Russian this way."

"I'm terrible at languages," Frost told her honestly.

"Are you trying to—"

"I don't know, really," Frost answered her. "Maybe just reflex action."

"If the Americans think of something—it will be very dangerous," she smiled, then the smile faded. "Very dangerous. Doomed, perhaps."

"I've been doomed since the day I was born—we all are. If I let being doomed stop me, well—hell, I don't know. I can't stay here all the rest of my life, can I? And just take language lessons. It's funny—but sometimes in America, well—there'll be ads in magazines, or in newspapers. For language lessons. But they don't mean that. Other things."

"What kind of other things?" she asked softly.

"I never paid for it in my life," he laughed, then felt awkward having said it.

"Paid for it?"

"The language lessons. They don't have anything to do with talking."

"Oh, I see, I think. They are—*zabahvnee?* Amusement?"

"I guess it depends on what amuses you," Frost answered thoughtfully. "Yeah, I guess so."

"And you wish to talk to me about this—this amusement? That is why you say I am—"

"Exquisite," Frost repeated.

"Yes, exquisite."

"Yes, exquisite," he told her. "But—ah—"

There was a knock at the door, then the door into the library opened.

It was Mr. Heath. "I say—hope not to be interrupting anything?"

"No, just *zabahvnee,*" Frost answered.

"Amusement," Arika Gorki echoed.

Heath said nothing for a moment.

Chapter Ten

Frost read the letter, having read it already five times at least. Bess was safe, doing all she could to help effect his release and—reading between the lines—worried she would never see him again. She had tried, against his wishes, to gain an entry visa to Russia, to see him at least. But it had been denied. Frost, despite the fact he wanted to see her desperately, was glad for it. If she had gained an entry visa, he doubted she would have been allowed to leave; more likely she would be implicated by the KGB in some sort of set-up to force him to surrender to them.

He put away the letter, standing up, stretching. He was bored, tired, stiff, and feeling generally useless. The CIA man, Crane, was coming soon—Frost checked his watch. The CIA man would be coming through the Embassy gates. He was prompt to the point of the ridiculous.

Frost pushed his feet into his sixty-five-dollar shoes and stood up. "Rats," he murmured, then started across the suite of rooms he used and toward the hall door.

He stepped out, into the corridor, then walked along its length toward the stairs.

He stopped halfway down the staircase, Crane standing at the bottom.

"You're late, Frost," Crane snapped.

"You're not," Frost smiled back. Frost continued down the stairs.

"You been taking your walks every morning in the courtyard?"

"Yeah," Frost nodded, lighting a cigarette as he reached the bottom of the staircase.

"Good—good for your health, too."

"I've been thinkin' about my health—a lot," Frost nodded. "My health requires a little more freedom of movement."

"Does it? What's ya got in mind?"

"Escape—from here, from Russia."

"You know the risks as well as I do," Crane snapped, walking toward the library. Frost followed Crane through the double wooden doors. "You're gonna miss your walk," Crane added.

"I'll take it later," Frost told him.

"You're taking it now. Take a look, but stay well away from the windows."

Frost followed Crane toward the library windows which overlooked the walled garden behind the Embassy building itself. Snow covered some of the stone work, and rather than green as a garden should be, in the Russian winter it was gray. The one-eyed man peered along the far edge of the garden, then stopped. His eye came to rest on a man, his own height, dressed in clothes similar to his own; the man had an eyepatch covering the left eye and a slouch hat pulled down over his face—the hat identical to the one Mr. Heath had given Frost a week earlier.

"That's you," Crane smiled. "Sort of a trial run. If the Russians don't seem to notice the difference over the next week, we make a try for it. He'll keep walking and you'll be running."

Frost dropped his cigarette into the pedestal ashtray beside the windows. "You've been—"

"It's not your golden personality, Captain, but the information you claim to have. But I'll tell you this, Frost. When you reach Langley—if you reach Langley—you'd better have something real great to talk about. Otherwise, you're gonna wish you'd stayed nice and cozy with the KGB in their little hospital?"

"A week?" Frost asked, ignoring Crane's thinly veiled threat.

"You practice your Russian—I'll tell you when. But there isn't much time. And remember, your chances of getting out alive are so slim it doesn't even pay to work the odds."

"*Spaseeba,*" Frost murmured.

"You're welcome," Crane nodded. "What's the Russian word for maybe?"

Crane walked away before Frost could even try to answer.

The one-eyed man stubbed out his cigarette that was still burning in the ashtray, then lit another one. "Oh, boy," he sighed.

Chapter Eleven

"A gun or I don't go—period," Frost insisted.

"A gun will give us away," Arika said suddenly.

Frost turned in his chair, looked at her over his shoulder. "Us?"

Crane answered, but Frost still looked at Arika Gorki. "She's more than a language instructor for us. She's one of our best contract agents. She's getting you out. If she can't, no one can."

Frost looked at Arika still, saying, "Crane, I take a gun or no go. Period. It is in character for me—the KGB will expect me to be armed. If I do get nailed, they'll treat me like I am armed. I don't wanna go down easy," and he turned finally and looked at Crane.

"Agreed—and you get this too." Crane reached into his attache case, the case on Heath's desk. Heath was sitting down, Crane standing beside him. Crane placed two revolvers on the desk and between them a small, gray capsule.

"Cyanide capsule?"

"Yeah, you just bite down on it—hard."

"Wonderful," the one-eyed man murmured. "What's the plan?" Frost studied Crane's face in the yellow lamplight from Heath's desk. He didn't like what he saw.

"Ever hear of Helen Keller?"

"Courageous lady," Frost nodded.

"She was deaf, dumb and blind. That's how you get out of Russian—the only way. Arika here—she'll be your niece. Your Russian accent sucks; you're already missing one eye and that can't be hidden or disguised without major cosmetic surgery."

"What?" Frost interrupted. "This sounds like a low budget escape?"

"No—it's the only way possible. We smuggle a cosmetic surgeon in here, the Russians are gonna know about it, seal the country up tighter than a drum."

"How tight is a drum?" Frost smiled.

It was Heath who spoke. "Captain Frost, we've talked often since your arrival here. I think I understand you better than anyone in this room—and in this instance perhaps better than you might even understand yourself. I wasn't always a diplomat. For several years I held a job similar to that which Mr. Crane holds now—with Her Majesty's Government, of course. I sent men out to do things that were—frightening. And I knew full well that in many instances I'd never see the men again. There was one man—the name doesn't really matter," and Heath smiled, then added, "I suppose it rarely does. He was a rather nondescript chap, intentionally so. And he had a good sense of humor. It was a particularly dangerous job, but a job that wanted doing badly. He did the job—and he never came back. But I remember when I briefed him. I believed then and I believe it now—that he somehow knew he wasn't going to make it. He joked. You Americans have an expression for it—laughing on the outside and—"

"Yeah," and the one-eyed man lit another cigarette, realizing then he already had one lit.

He stood up, picked up one of the twin revolvers from the desk. It was a blued Smith & Wesson Model 15, the

Combat Masterpiece .38 Special revolver. There were no markings on it, serial or origin. "Marines?" Frost asked Crane absently.

"Once," the CIA man nodded.

"Once," Frost agreed.

Chapter Twelve

Crane had told him that the mental hospital where Frost would likely have been sent was in Siberia, actually one of the nicer portions. As a Siberian alternative, escaping Russia by way of Riga in what had been Latvia seemed positively inviting, even disguised as a blind and deaf mute.

Frost had practiced the role for nearly a week, moving about with dark glasses through which he could not see. Arika had coached him, worked with him, dropping a cigarette on his hand once to see if Frost would cry out. But Frost had only made a grunting sound. She had said to him, "You should have been an actor."

Frost had taken off the dark glasses, looked at her and said, "Hardly," then drawn the woman into his arms. It was neither passion nor infidelity, he had reasoned—it was cold, reason. To trust this woman was his only means of survival, and to trust her he had to know her. He had kissed her lightly once and she had edged away, then handed him the glasses.

He had put them back on, then continued practicing being blind—but another sense was operative now, a feeling about the woman Arika. And it had made him nervous. . . .

Frost checked the two revolvers. The loads in them were only the rather poor performing 158-grain Round Nosed Lead service loads. There were twenty-four extra rounds, twelve for each gun, and with the twelve loaded in the two revolvers, a total of thirty-six rounds. "This *is* a low-budget escape," Frost told Crane.

"Hiding two revolvers and some spare ammo will be hard enough—more ammo than that and you'd just increase the problem."

"I'd still like it if you left the guns behind—you won't need them, and if you do—"

"They won't help," Frost interrupted her. "I know. But they're never capturing me again."

"Here," and Crane handed Frost the cyanide capsule. There was a small pouch cut in the inside of Frost's trouser band and Frost inserted the pill there, then closed the tiny hook and pile fastener over it. Crane, for the first time since Frost had met him, smiled. "Hey, look. I hope you make it. Not just for the information. I really hope you make it."

Crane extended his hand and Frost took it. "Thank you. I'll buy you dinner when you come back to the States."

"Deal," Crane said—Frost thought—too soberly.

"Please, leave the guns," Arika asked once more.

Frost looked at her, feeling coldness in his eye. "No."

"Good luck, old boy," Heath smiled suddenly, taking Frost's right hand and patting him roundly on the right shoulder. "You'll need it. But I've become convinced on one point at least. If anyone can make it out, you can."

Frost smiled, nodding. "Mr. Heath, you ever need somebody's legs broken, well—you just call."

"Beautifully put, dear boy. And," Heath smiled, "I'd certainly think of you."

The one-eyed man glanced at his surroundings—the back door of the Embassy, the service entrance. Once he put on the glasses, aside from a little peripheral vision on his right side, he would see nothing.

"Here are your papers," Crane said then. "Travel permits, identity papers—all of it. Arika will carry them."

"Forged?"

"No—we got them another way," Crane said non-committally. "They're perfect. If you can convince everyone around you you're blind and deaf and can't speak, these papers'll get you to Riga. After that—well, Arika knows."

"Submarine?" Frost asked.

"Yeah, but Arika will give you the details when you need them," Crane said with an air of finality.

"All right," Frost nodded, securing the guns inside the waistband of his baggy trousers.

"The wristwatch, Captain," Heath smiled.

Frost nodded, removing the Rolex from his left wrist, handing it to Heath. "Not just what it cost, but sentimental value."

"The diplomatic pouch will get through—and everything will be returned to you," Heath smiled.

Frost nodded, knowing that it would. Heath already had his wallet, his money clip, his keys, his cigarette lighter; everything he now possessed had been given to the man. In exchange for two pairs of black-painted glasses, a pair of baggy work pants, a scratchy woolen shirt, a sweater with a patched left elbow and a heavy mid-thigh length coat, the coat patched in several places. Frost, his hair dyed gray and parted on the opposite side, caught a glimpse of his face in the full-length mirror in the back hall as he removed his eyepatch, handing that too to Heath. His mustache was gone, replacing it the stubble of four days' growth of beard, the beard already gray enough that it hadn't had to be dyed.

"All right, gentlemen," he smiled, putting on the glasses. Without looking at her, he said to the Gorki woman, "Arika, I'm ready."

The one-eyed man hated starting a venture on a lie.

Chapter Thirteen

Frost held his breath, for fear that the guards—whose voices he now heard—would somehow hear him. He reached out in the darkness, holding against the seat cushion spring. Above him, on the other side of the hollowed seat back, sat Arika and beside her—on the side that sagged more—sat Crane, the CIA man.

Frost knew enough of the language now to give himself a running semi-translation. The guard—one of them—was asking Crane if the man had had a pleasant evening at the British Embassy. Crane was answering that diplomatic functions were always the same—tedious.

Arika laughed once, saying then that she rather enjoyed a party. It was a dull life being a teacher of Russian language.

Another voice—perhaps the chauffeur or another guard—said something about papers that Frost didn't quite follow, then Frost heard the engine gunning to life again, the Cadillac's transmission being shifted, and he began again to feel the motion. He had never in his life been carsick, but riding folded like a discarded accordion under the rear seat of an automobile was starting to change that. He imagined himself smelling exhaust fumes.

He looked to his wrist, for the luminous black face of the Rolex Sea Dweller, then realized he had left the watch with Heath and had no timepiece. What reason would a blind man have for wearing one?

The ride seemed interminable, but then suddenly Frost heard the popping sound—one of the tires blowing, the car swerving. The carsickness welled up in the one-eyed man as the car lurched, skidded, and came to a halt.

He heard the door slam, heard a sound from above him, as if Arika had whispered something to Crane, or perhaps the other way around.

He felt the cold rush of air and heard the sound of the trunk lid opening.

"I'll have to change the tire, sir," the chauffeur's voice clearly sounded.

"Be quick about it, Harrison," Crane shouted back. "Got a phone call to make from my office within the next twenty minutes."

"Right, Mr. Crane. Hey, looks like we've got a motorist stopping. Maybe I can use his lights."

Frost decided neither Crane nor Harrison, the chauffeur and bodyguard, would win an award for believable acting. The car was part of the plan, the most important part, assuming Crane would be watched by the KGB.

A Russian voice, speaking in poor English. "The automobile—it does not drive?"

"A flat, a puncture—you know," the chauffeur's voice came back.

"Ploeskee?"

"Right—a flat," the chauffeur answered.

"I will help this," the Russian-accented voice answered, a man Frost guessed somewhere in middle age.

"Thank you," the chauffeur answered with a total lack of spontaneity.

Frost could hear it, the spare tire being removed, and the banging of something against the inside of the trunk—three times, then once more. It was the signal.

Frost saw the lights of the headlights, off to his right, the car parked at an angle to the Cadillac's trunk.

"Go," the chauffeur rasped, and Frost, banging his head on the trunk lid, stepped out onto the icy street. Slipping, catching himself, he then stumbled toward the back seat of the car—he thought it was a Moscvitch.

He fell across the floor between the front and rear seat, hearing a woman's voice saying, "I cover you with this blanket."

Frost breathed again. But he could feel himself sweat—the scenario called for the driver of the Moscvitch to continue helping Harrison the chauffeur until the tire was changed. Frost mentally counted the seconds. "One thousand one, one thousand two, one thousand three—" It took seven and a half minutes from the time he started counting, but seemed an eternity.

There were exchanges of pleasantries, some in Russian, some in English, then a loud and stagey-sounding, "Thank you again," from Harrison and Frost heard a car door open and slam shut, then the sound of the Moscvitch's engine rumbling to life.

"You are on your way, my friend," the same voice said, but this time the English was perfect. "Now be very silent and pray a lot," the voice added. "The KGB has been parked across the street for the last four and one-half minutes."

"Shit," Frost rumbled, feeling the car starting to move. . . .

* * *

The one-eyed man sat quietly in a strange room, smoking a Russian cigarette, the name of which he couldn't remember, the large filter cut off with a table knife. He had read somewhere that Soviet cigarettes were made with long filters because the climate was so cold in the winter the long filter enabled the smoker to more easily hold the cigarette while wearing heavy gloves. It made sense, Frost mused, if you liked filters.

The driver of the Moscvitch re-entered the room. "There has been a delay in Miss Gorki getting away from the American Embassy—the KGB is watching it more tightly than usual."

"You think they suspect?" Frost asked.

"Of course they suspect—the KGB always suspects. But do they suspect something specific? That is the question," the man offered.

"Then," and Frost paused, stubbing out the cigarette, "do they suspect something specific?"

"I think not. There has been no roundup of the usual suspects as far as I am able to determine. You had best resign yourself to staying with us for a time, at least a few hours, Captain Frost."

"What's your name?"

"Names are not useful when I engage in this line of work. You can call me Ivan if you like. It is not my real name, but I will answer to it."

"Do I gather from talking with you there's a formalized anti-Communist underground in Moscow?"

"You may gather what you like." Ivan smiled, sitting down opposite Frost at the smallish table in the center of the parlor.

"And this," Frost went on. "A private home, a car. You're well off."

"Yes—as the average Soviet citizen goes, I am well off. I could hardly have brought you to a communal apartment complex, could I?"

"A professional man, perhaps a scientist?"

Ivan laughed. Frost had heard little laughter in the Soviet Union. "Hardly—mathematics was my worst subject at the University. No—but your curiosity seems insatiable, and if you press you will doubtless find some clue to my real identity, and that could be fatal for myself and for my family. So I ask, no more questions, please. For the welfare of us all."

"Agreed," the one-eyed man nodded. "You got anything to eat around here?" Frost smiled. "Sorry—that was another question."

"Food—yes, and I apologize for not mentioning it. My wife is already preparing something for you."

"One more question—because I assume you've helped in things like this before," Frost began.

Ivan smiled non-committally. "What is this one so pregnant question, then?"

"Do you think I have a chance?"

"No. But you must try, just as all of us must try," and Ivan stood, then walked to the mantelpiece, taking down a fifth-sized bottle of vodka. "A drink. I'm sure the Americans have heard of vodka."

Frost smiled. "I recall hearing it mentioned." He refrained from asking for orange juice. . . .

Frost opened his eye—it was dark again. He had spent almost twenty-four hours as the uncomfortable guest of "Ivan" and his nameless wife. Ivan had advised Frost get all the sleep possible, because once the run started, there would be little time, if any, for it. Frost had agreed, sleeping surprisingly well. He decided the fear and tension had somehow exhausted him.

He heard a knocking at the door of the bedroom, then remembered that the knocking sound had been what he'd heard in his sleep, what had at first awakened him.

"Yes," he said.

The door opened, a narrow shaft of yellow light penetrating the darkness of the room. It was Ivan's wife who spoke. "Captain Frost, my husband wishes to speak with you. It is urgent."

"All right," and Frost sat up, reaching in the darkness for the small lamp he remembered as being beside the bed. He almost knocked it over, but found it, pulling the antiquated chain.

He sat over the side, his legs stiff, his feet cold against the bare floor. He found his one pair of socks—they were stiff and smelled—and pulled them on, then stepped into his low black boots.

He stood, walked across the room, then opened the door and went into the hallway, the faded wallpaper there giving the hall a grayish tinge. Everything in Russia seemed gray.

Ivan was waiting beside the mantelpiece, the vodka bottle in his hand. "A drink, Captain?"

Frost looked at his wrist, then remembered he wore no watch. "Will I need one?"

"The KGB knows that you have escaped the British Embassy, and somehow that you were supposed to be disguised as a blind man. Your travel papers and identity papers are useless."

"What about Arika Gorki?"

"She had disappeared from the American Embassy and may even now be heading here. Now—about the drink, Captain?"

Frost nodded.

"I cannot surrender—I'm a Soviet national. I'd be tried for espionage, then executed. Or worse," said the woman. She had made it to Ivan's, barely.

"Like they had planned for me?" Frost asked her.

"Yes—or worse still. I saw an American movie once," Arika Gorki said, looking away at the sunlight through the window of the parlor. "There was a Nazi officer in the movie, and he said to the hero who had been captured, 'We have ways of making even the strongest person beg to tell us what we want to know.' The KGB has such ways, too, I think."

Somewhere, somehow, Frost felt something very big was wrong. Not the lapse in security, wherever it had originated, not the useless identity and travel papers, not Arika Gorki now being wanted as well. Something more than that, something more subtle.

The one-eyed man had changed into clothes borrowed—permanently—from Ivan. He had showered, washing the gray coloring from his hair, shaved, leaving only the usually drooping mustache, and taken the eyepatch he had secreted in his "old man" outfit and put it on. The two .38 Special revolvers stuffed in his trouser belt, one behind the bone of each hip, butts forward, wearing a dark blue turtleneck sweater and dark gray workpants, heavy boots with clean socks, he felt almost himself. Except for his watch and his other things.

"We're going anyway," Frost told her.

"I assumed you'd say that," Ivan smiled. "It was as though you were a knight, suiting up for battle this morning. The old man disappeared and you emerged after your bath. You will never make it."

"I've got two guns and some ammunition. Maybe I can get your wife to give me a butcher knife. If I don't make it, I'll go down trying. I can't surrender."

"I will help all that I can, as will my wife," Ivan nodded.

Frost looked at Arika. "What did Crane say—when he knew the Russians were onto you?"

"That I was a fool to attempt to leave. But that if I

found you, I should advise you to somehow make it back to the American Embassy. At least you would be safe there."

"How'd you get out?" Frost asked her.

"I changed clothes with the cleaning lady—used pillows to stuff her dress. It was rather simple. I knocked out the cleaning lady."

"Why?"

"Escape. To be free—like you. That is all. You are free now. You will probably die, but when you left the British Embassy, you became a free man again. I am a free woman. That is all."

"Can you still contact the submarine?"

"Yes—I think it will be there anyway, in case you should make it that far."

"They will know that route," Ivan offered.

"So they won't expect us to use it," Frost told him. Then, "Do you know where the normal checkpoints are along the road?"

"Of course—but that will do you no good. There will be added checkpoints, and if you go cross country—which in this weather would be insane—you will encounter patrols, guard dogs, every obstacle imaginable."

"Good," Frost nodded abruptly. "Patrols mean a ready source of rations if we need them, guns, ammunition, changes of clothing."

"You intend to kill your way across the Soviet Union to the Baltic!"

"Yes," the one-eyed man answered. He felt himself smiling. "Couldn't be a better spot for it, could there?"

Frost belted down a glass of the vodka—it burned his throat and his insides.

Chapter Fourteen

"Moscow to Minsk, then on to Vilna, then to Riga—but that is insane even to think of. We shall not make it that far," the woman said.

Frost felt himself smiling as he closed his coat over the two pistols. "Think positive, kid—we'll make it." He wished he believed it himself.

"Papers—we—"

"Puppies need papers, not free human beings," Frost told her flatly.

He turned to Ivan. "I don't know your real name, but no matter what happens, I'll—"

"If they catch you, you will tell them everything you know eventually. You will have no choice. But our prayers are with you that they do not. And—the thought is something I appreciate."

Frost only nodded, turning, taking Arika's hand and starting with her down the back steps of the house. There was a postage stamp-sized yard, snow covered, and beyond it an open wooded area. They crossed through the gate into the woods, and when Frost turned around "Ivan" and his wife were gone.

"We'll never make it," Arika Gorki repeated.

Frost didn't bother to answer it. He started off instead

toward the deep part of the woods. . . .

The truck was slowing, stopping. Frost had used the ploy once—twice as a matter of fact—in Africa when he'd first met Bess.* Arika lay in the middle of the road, motionless, having lain there long enough that the falling snow had covered her coat. There was a chance, in fact, she might not be seen.

But the truck did stop, two Soviet soldiers climbing out, both armed with AKM rifles, both holding the rifles in an assault position.

The man from the driver's side was nearer to Arika and bent over her.

Arika rolled, the pistol coming up in her right fist, firing, pointblank into the soldier's face. There was a scream, but the last portion of the scream was drowned out, Frost stepping from the bracken of snow-laden pines, the second of the two Combat Masterpieces in his right fist. His first finger twitched against the trigger and the second man's body lurched forward, the arms flying out from the rifle, the rifle falling into the snow, the body dropping face first into the snow.

"Ha," Frost smiled. Not at the death. He had never grown to like killing, but he smiled rather at his success. Two dead soldiers meant a truck, two uniforms, and two assault rifles at the least.

"They are—they are—"

"Dead," Frost concluded, still standing more than a dozen yards from Arika, Arika on her knees in the snow, holding her revolver limply in her right hand.

Frost walked toward the nearest of the bodies, the man he had shot. He felt himself growing more clinical in his old age—that is, his middle thirties. He assessed the wound, the 158-grain round-nosed lead having penetrated at the back of the skull, the lead bullet apparently

*See *They Call Me the Mercenary #1: Killer Genesis*

having done its work. There was no exit wound, no sign of much bleeding. The lead had apparently struck the bone, mushroomed—uncharacteristic of the solid—and dropped the man.

Frost opened his coat, shoving the pistol into his belt. "Help me get the uniforms off them, then we'll bury 'em in a snowdrift. Leave their dogtags or whatever so their next of kin can be notified. Just in case animals get to them."

He heard the sound, then turned and confirmed what he'd heard. She'd thrown up....

Dressed as a Soviet corporal—the rank was getting monotonous, he thought—Frost began inspecting the truck, while Arika changed. He threw back the tarp cover and climbed inside. The one-eyed man smiled. He couldn't read the Cyrillic, but the emblem emblazoned on each of the crates told him what the cargo was—explosives.

"Arika—what the hell does a little squiggle under something that looks like a—"

"You don't have to shout."

Frost turned around, the woman standing behind him but still on the road side outside the truck. "It means," she said, "—the whole inscription I mean—it means what you call plastique. Plastique explosives."

"Ignition wires will work as detonator wires in a pinch—or so will a bullet. All right. We're in business."

Frost glanced at the cheap Soviet wristwatch he wore, realizing they'd been parked along the roadside for almost seven minutes. "We're pushin' it. Let's get the hell out of here."

The one-eyed man jumped down from the back of the truck. Aside from a wristwatch, the dead man with whom he'd changed clothes had also had a pack of American cigarettes—Winstons. He smiled as he closed the tarp. If he killed somebody else who smoked, he hoped the guy would have his brand.

As they drove now, the girl looking over the map, Frost asked her, "You feelin' better, kid?"

"I never killed anyone before."

"You don't get used to it, you just get sick in private," Frost told her, smoking one of the cigarettes he'd stolen.

"It bothers you, then—killing?"

"Yeah, but I do it when it needs to be done. Anybody killing doesn't bother one way or another—well, they're dead themselves. But you do it anyway. Self-preservation. You'll make it."

"What are you going to do with the explosives?"

"I've already done it," Frost told her. "When we stopped an hour back for you to go answer nature? I opened a few of the crates, found detonators and wire. I rigged the truck," and Frost reached down beside the front seat and lifted two wires in his left hand. The ends of the wires were stripped back, one of the wires taped. "This wire's connected into the ignition system, the other one to the explosives and the detonator. We get in trouble, all I do is goose the ignition switch and we've got juice. All I have to do is link the two wires together."

"But that would kill us as well."

"More than likely, but not necessarily. Best way to use the explosives I could think of. We get stopped and cornered, they'll never capture us and we'll take a whole pile of them with us."

Frost felt his smile freeze. There was a checkpoint ahead and already stopped beside the official cars making the roadblock was an army truck, identical to the one they drove. "Shit," Frost murmured.

He began slowing the truck, glancing in the sideview mirror to see if there were any way of escape. The papers would never stand scrutiny, and if the military truck ahead were being searched, it could only mean the drivers of the truck whom Frost and the girl had killed had been missed. The number designations on the truck would instantly finger them.

"They are looking for us," the girl said, her voice sounding tight, afraid. "There should not be a checkpoint here, not for miles."

Frost had taken the truck to the highway because the snow on the side, dirt roads he had driven, had become too deep. The wiper blades ticked and tocked, sweeping back and forth, their noise maddening as they scraped the snow away. The one-eyed man's mind raced.

He glanced into the sideview mirror again, then stomped on the brake pedal, his left foot working the clutch as he wrenched the stick across into second. "We're getting out of here," he rasped, starting to turn the wheel hard left, the truck moving.

The girl almost screamed the words, "We'll never make it!"

"Bullshit!" Frost cranied the transmission into third as he came out of the tight turn, the truck bogging down on the far shoulder opposite the lane he'd just left, the snow there deeper than he'd thought. He glanced into the passenger side sideview mirror—already military vehicles and unmarked cars were skidding across the road toward them. "Dammit," he rasped, wrenching the stick down into second, double clutching, the truck moving again. Frost stomped the clutch, double clutching with the gas pedal as he upshifted, the truck bouncing out of the drifts on the shoulder and back onto the road surface.

He hit the wiper blade switch moving to the higher speed, slush washing up in a wave across the hood now as he hit a massive pothole, the truck skidding, but still under control. The one-eyed man fought the wheel, straightening out the massive truck beneath him, driving it now down the center of the highway.

A police car of some sort was coming at him, almost head on from the opposite lane.

The one-eyed man felt himself smile. The car swerved to avoid the truck, Frost swerving the truck to hit the car. He knocked it off the road and onto the shoulder, the car rolling over. "Chalk up one," Frost almost shouted.

"Stop—they'll kill us!"

"Hang on," he rasped, downshifting, cutting the wheel into a hard left, pulling up on the emergency brake, the truck skidding wildly, in a tight circle. Frost released the brake and dropped all the way down into first, giving the truck gas, slowly, then increasing it as he fought the wheel; upshifting, double clutching as he did, the truck straightened now.

"Here we go," he snarled. The military and police cars were coming toward him, cutting across the opposite lane now as Frost hammered down the clutch, stomped the gas, upshifted, then let out the clutch. The truck's engine roared now, the rear end fishtailing slightly on the snow and ice. "Come on, baby," he cooed. "Come on."

There was a green-brown military car coming head on, a man leaning out from the back seat, an assault rifle in his hands. "Shoot at him, Arika," Frost ordered.

The one-eyed man cut the wheel hard left, straight toward the military car. "Shoot at him!"

The woman beside him now was lifting her rifle, cranking down the window, ramming the rifle through the opening. "Shoot," Frost shouted.

He heard the popping sound of the first round, then the long, unending banging as she fired out the magazine, the muzzle of the weapon rising as Frost glanced toward her.

The military car swerved right, Frost cutting the

wheel of the truck right, the rear end of the truck fishtailing. He heard the impact, felt it, glancing into the rearview, the military car's bumper locked against the rear wheel well of the truck.

Frost downshifted, the car still locked to the truck. "Shit!"

The one-eyed man wrenched the wheel hard right, then hard left, intentionally fishtailing the truck, but the military car was still locked to the truck's rear end. Gunfire was coming from the car, the man in the back seat still firing.

Frost reached under his uniform tunic, snatching one of the revolvers. If the gunfire hit the plastique, the entire cargo would explode.

Frost rammed the revolver out the window in his right fist, turning awkwardly for the shot, holding the wheel cross body with his left, the Smith & Wesson revolver bucking once, then once more in his right fist. The gunfire was still coming, the sideview mirror shattering inches from Frost's face.

The truck was skidding now. Frost steadied the muzzle as best he could across his left shoulder, the hammer cocking back under his right thumb, Frost trying to judge the sway, the up and down motion as his finger took up the slack. As the sights settled he snapped the trigger back, the revolver bucking up. A burst of automatic weapons fire came from the back seat of the car. The door opened suddenly and a uniformed man's body rolled out onto the road surface, the wheels of the car, being dragged diagonally behind the truck, crushing him. There was a wailing scream for less than a second, then the body was gone.

Frost wrenched the wheel of the truck hard left, avoiding the shoulder and the deep snow there, the truck skidding now, a wrenching and tearing sound of metal against metal. He glanced behind him, awkwardly over his left shoulder; the military automobile broke free, whiplashing across the highway into the oncoming lanes and two police cars trying to pursue.

"Ha!" The one-eyed man suddenly realized there was the filter tip of a dead cigarette in his lips. He spat it out the window, then hammered down on the gas pedal, double clutching as he upshifted into fourth gear, the road block dead ahead.

"Drop down to the floor boards, kid," he snapped, not looking at Arika as he spoke.

He made two rounds remaining in the revolver as he lifted it from the seat, then shifted it to his left hand.

He stabbed the revolver out his window, firing as he closed the distance on the barricade—two fast shots. He hit a policeman standing beside one of the cars. There was answering gunfire, Frost dodging instinctively as the windshield shattered in front of his face, bits and pieces of broken glass showering him, the truck swerving under him.

He recovered the wheel, hitting the barricade now. "Keep down," he snapped. The left front fender of the truck slammed hard against the front of the police car beside which the now dead man had stood. Frost worked the stick, downshifting for more power, the truck slowing, then lurching ahead as it punched through. The police cars blocked it but, peeling away, Frost continued to downshift. He stomped the brake pedal, wrenching up on the emergency brake as he did, throwing himself across the front seat as the remainder of the glass shattered inward under a burst of automatic weapons fire. He reached back, ripping the tape from the ignition wire. The detonator he'd set in the plastique was a sixty-second delay. He wrapped the two wires together, then turned the ignition switch.

"Come on," and the one-eyed man wrenched open the passenger side door handle, slid across the seat.

Pushing the girl ahead of him, he hurtled both the girl and himself into the snowbank at the side of the road.

Automatic weapons fire poured toward him. The one-eyed man dropped to his knees, firing a long burst from the AKM assault rifle, then he pushed the girl up and, getting to his feet, he ran with her. Frost was counting seconds. "One thousand fifty-six, one thousand fifty-seven.

"Run! Run!" He had her left hand in his right, gunfire from the barricade chewing into the snow around them.

"One thousand sixty!" he shouted, then dragged the girl down into the snow, throwing his body across hers.

He got his hands to his ears, but the sound was still deafening. The ground beneath them trembled, the girl starting to scream, but the scream was drowned out in the noise of the explosion.

He could feel debris—some of it hot—pelting at the exposed skin on the back of his neck, on his hands. Something hard hammered into his right thigh and he could feel himself shout in anguish, but he could hear nothing.

The pelting of his body stopped. His ears rang and he could hear nothing, not even the sound of his own breathing.

He pushed himself up, his right leg hurting him. He glanced down toward his leg, a large piece of automobile—perhaps a fender or a part of a door panel; it was so twisted and mangled he couldn't recognize it—fell away to the gray and red-splotched snow.

There was no sign of a wound on his leg and as he stood fully erect, he flexed the leg, trying to ease the pain.

The girl was saying something, then was screaming, tears coming down her white cheeks. But Frost couldn't hear her, his ears still ringing.

But he knew why she was screaming.

All the police and military vehicles had closed around the truck, and the men who had been firing at them had been concentrated there as well. It was as if everything in the area—man and machine—had been vaporized. The wind was blowing hard, Frost feeling it against his skin but not hearing it. It would be hours before his hearing returned to normal, he knew.

Flames flickered from charred hunks of debris, some of the charred hunks once human. Nothing lived.

Frost rammed a fresh magazine into his assault rifle, then glanced back down the road.

The military vehicle he had dragged behind the truck, then whiplashed into two police cars, all of them crashed. It was still upright. Perhaps he could make it run again.

He took the girl's hand to start toward it, but she pulled away. She was screaming something at him. He couldn't hear, but he had watched her mouth so carefully over the time she had worked with him, teaching him Russian, that he could lip-read her. He was almost certain she was screaming, "Murderer!"

Chapter Fifteen

The stolen military car, wrecked partially, had gotten them near enough to Minsk that in what Frost would have labeled a suburb, he had been able to steal still another car. Because of the snow, Vilna had been another hard day's ride, harder still because of the care with which they selected roadways.

After stealing the car, Frost had broken and entered a small department store, smashing through a carelessly assembled display window, grabbing an armful of women's clothing for Arika and a man's jacket for himself.

His military uniform tunic discarded, both revolvers stuffed in his trouser belt, he stood now beside the car, then turned to Arika. "You think we should shoot it—put it out of its misery?"

"I am not amused," the woman answered, then turned away. Of all the clothes Frost had stolen for her, she had found one dress that fit her reasonably well and two pairs of slacks and one blouse. She wore the dress now.

"You'd better change if we're gonna walk it."

"Do you know how far it still is to Riga? And we are in the middle of—of nowhere! With no car!"

"Remind me never to travel with you again," Frost told her acidly. "We've got a contact Ivan gave us—in Riga, right?"

"If we ever get there—and we won't now. We'll just freeze to death out here."

"Here, have a Hershey bar. Found 'em in the glove compartment. Saving 'em for a time like this," and he reached into his pocket, producing two of the chocolate bars, giving her one.

"How can you eat at a time like this?"

"Always had a weakness for Hershey bars. Only candy I like." Frost unwrapped the chocolate and broke off a chunk. He kept it in his mouth as he talked, liking the taste. "See—I'm on a roll now, kid. I'll steal us another car or something. Get us to Riga. Then we just find that submarine."

"It will be gone. We should have been there two days ago. I'm tired." She began to cry.

"Come here," said Frost. He folded the woman—hysterical—into his arms. She wept so loudly, her body shuddering, he felt sorry for her. It was a new emotion to him, concerning her.

There was still gas in the car and he started it, taking her in beside him onto the front seat. The car knocked loudly and Frost assumed they had damaged the engine somehow when the axle had broken. There was a window partially open though, and he didn't fear they would die of asphyxiation. Nearing darkness, they could stay in the car for a while where it was warm while he plotted their next move.

He felt her hands—they were opening his jacket.

"Make love to me," she murmured, still crying.

The one-eyed man kissed her, her lips trembling slightly.

It was somehow different for him, living with Bess, different than it had been. He loved her no differently, no more really and certainly no less. But living with her, it somehow made—

He felt Arika's hands exploring his chest under his sweater. It wasn't a rationalization—despite her beauty, making love to her was something that somehow he didn't want to do. But several things had bothered him. One of the things was the woman herself. A spy, or agent—or whatever term seemed best—she was a native Russian and worked for the CIA; and Crane had ironed out an escape plan which he had felt confident enough to have Frost try. Yet it had all gone wrong. The girl had escaped from the American Embassy with the KGB watching outside, and together they had driven and run nearly all the way to the Baltic Coast. To "defeat" the KGB on their home turf was, he had known from the start, an impossibility or virtually so. And now she wanted to make love. It was as if she turned herself on and off, hating him one moment, cowardly, then alternately courageous and wanting him.

He cupped his left hand against her right breast, kissing her mouth hard.

The engine of the automobile still ran, and it was warm in the car, so warm that after they had crawled into the back seat together, she had had him remove her clothes. Naked, the dress she'd worn under her against the rough surface of the seat, her body moved under him now, his fingers exploring the erect nipples of her breasts, touching at them, his eye watching her quiver when he did. His naked rear end felt cold as he pushed down his pants, slipping as gracefully as he could between her thighs, feeling the warmth of her against his own cold, her hands touching him, making the hardness come as he raised her up slightly, arcing the small of her back, feeling her hands guiding him into her. She shuddered, her body moving under his, so rhythmically and unbroken at once that he could feel something happening to him.

"Hank," the woman murmured in his ear, the one-eyed man closing his eye, pain consuming him, building in him.

He could feel his body start to tremble, hers trembling in perfect rhythm with his. She shuddered beneath him, murmuring words he couldn't understand—perhaps it was Russian. He couldn't tell; the words soft, cooed to him. A spasm racked his body and he sank against her, listening to her breathe.

A terrifying thought was now formulated in his mind, and the lovemaking had somehow confirmed it, in a way words could never have. He felt convinced he had made love to either the most accomplished woman he had ever made love to, or to someone who in some inexplicable way, was partially a machine.

The thought made the one-eyed man shiver.

Chapter Sixteen

They had walked, Frost decided, no more than two miles, and already his thighs were stiff with the cold, his mustache feeling frozen from condensation as he exhaled. Snow covered the landscape, the ground rolling gently in a vague contour downward toward, he guessed, Riga and the Baltic beyond. Had he been alone, he would have pressed on, so close to Riga now that risking the theft of still another vehicle was insanity. But the woman could go no further. He had no conception how large a city Riga was, but to attempt to walk across New York City or Chicago (muggings aside) would have been a trial in severe cold. A car—he had to have one.

"I can't go—"

It was the most defeated, the most depressed woman he had known—not the tempestuous woman who had made love with him. "I know," Frost told her, his teeth chattering when he opened his mouth to speak. "I'll climb that rise and see if there's anything in sight. Hang on," he added lamely. The one-eyed man started toward the low, snow-covered hill a hundred yards to his left, jogging to get circulation going into his legs and feet and arms again. At the base of the hill, he started to climb, the rise sharper, steeper than he had thought it would be—either that or his exhaustion telling on him more greatly than he had supposed.

He stopped, not daring to sit down lest he fall asleep and freeze—he had little faith in Arika aiding him. He shook his head, clearing it, then continued on.

Frost slumped forward at the top of the rise. Beyond the rise lay a barren, snowswept plain, and five hundred yards or so distant—no more certainly than a half mile—was a farmhouse. He could barely discern a plume of smoke rising from a chimney. And beside the house was a lean-to that looked like a stable. There were very few privately worked farms in the Soviet Union. He had found one. The difficult task would be getting there with Arika.

He had practiced flexing his right hand for the last hundred yards, so he could properly hold one of the two revolvers. To have fumbled with the AKM's safety in the flesh stiffening cold would have been out of the question.

He stopped, Arika leaning heavily beside him, sweating profusely, exhaustion taking her.

He reached out his stiff left hand and hammered on the door with his fist. There was no answer.

He hammered again. He saw, at a side window, the movement of a drab brown curtain.

He looked at the gun in his hand, then fumbled his left hand to the cylinder release catch, awkwardly pushing it forward, then simultaneously swinging out the cylinder. His right thumb barely moved. He stabbed at the ejector rod with the gloved palm of his left hand, the cartridges spilling out into the snow at his feet. He shoved the four-inch-barreled revolver into his pocket, then bent to pick up the cartridges. He could barely get them with the gloves on, but couldn't trust removing the gloves, nor did he want to see the color of the flesh underneath.

He tried to remember the word, the curtain still drawn back but no face visible.

"Pamagheetyeh!"

The word meant help. He closed his eye and hoped the door would open. There was nothing left to do for his fingers were too stiff to find the second revolver, let alone reload the first. . . .

"A little, I speak—I practice you, yes?"

"Yes," Frost smiled wearily. "Thank you," he added as he held the mug of tea in his hands, the heat from the mug perhaps enough to burn him, but the warmth pleasing to him regardless.

"The woman—he is—"

"She is," Frost corrected absently.

"She is the wife of you?" the woman asked.

"A friend—a friend," he repeated.

"Fred?"

"No—friend. *Drook,*" he repeated.

"*Drook!* Friend!"

"Yes," Frost told her.

"Americanshe?"

"Me? Yes," Frost nodded, seeing no sense in lying. "Wanted by the—the police," he told her.

"Politcia?"

"Yes—*politcia.*" He didn't know how to say KGB in Russian—the thought made him laugh.

"Bad—what did you?"

Frost shook his head, waiting for the last word of the question. It didn't come. "Escaped—from the police. Trying to go home."

The voice was hoarse sounding a little as the woman repeated, "Go home?"

He laughed, suddenly, hysterically, thinking perhaps he'd gone insane. Smiling, his face hurting with it, the one-eyed man said, "Frost go home."

He closed his eye, laughing, wanting to cry as well.

"Go home," the woman said with a smile when Frost finally opened his eye. "Away *politcia?*"

"Yes," Frost nodded.

She said something and he thought he caught the Russian word, "*Vahravat.*"

"Steal—I stole a car to get away—some other things."

"*Vahravat*—steal?"

"Yes," he nodded.

"Steal the car—please," and she smiled.

Frost shook his head, not understanding. The woman nodded, smiled, got up and walked off. He guessed her age somewhere around fifty. She was a little fat, her hair graying heavily, her skin leathery. He guessed it was the climate's effect on her skin.

"*Vahravat!*" She said it proudly as she returned, standing in front of him, and in her hand she held what looked like—keys.

"*Americanshe*—steal the car. Please?" She smiled again, adding, "Go home?"

As the one-eyed man took the keys from the woman, he kissed her hand.

Chapter Seventeen

He had tied up the woman's wrists and ankles, loosely enough that she could get herself free in minutes. She had suggested it. He had worried that alone on the farm she might be in danger without the old pickup-style truck. Her husband, she had said, would return the next morning from just outside Riga—with the tractor which had needed to be repaired. He was a Communist, she was not. She would tell him two Americans had broken into the house, tied her up and stolen the truck. He would believe that because he hated Americans. She did not.

As Frost tooled the old truck off the snow laden farm road and onto a two-lane highway toward Riga, he was happy she hadn't hated Americans.

"That old woman was risking her life," Arika commented.

"I know—you find that sometimes," Frost told her, lighting the last of the American cigarettes he had stolen from the driver of the explosives truck. "I usually make a living as a mercenary."

"I know that," she nodded as Frost glanced at her.

"Anyway, you sometimes can't understand something unless you've done it. Sometimes in the middle of hell, you meet the finest people. They just happen to be stuck there, just like you are. You know?"

"No, I don't," Arika said, looking away.

Frost glanced to the road, then back at her. He shook his head, then returned to studying the road ahead of him. From what the old woman had said, in three hours he should be at the coast. Three hours, then perhaps another few hours until contact was made with the submarine and although he'd be trapped in the same boat with her, he'd be rid of her. Arika Gorki was beginning to give him—he half-verbalized it—"the creeps. . . ." He shook his head and continued driving. . . .

They had circled the town of Riga, not once encountering a checkpoint, and now, standing beside Arika, Frost stared at the icy Baltic. Below him between the high rocks on which he stood and the sea lay a beach, a barbed wire fence stretched along its length as far as he could see. "Must be rough being a sunbather in the Soviet Union," he commented, wishing he had a cigarette.

"Only the unused beaches near enough to strategic locations are fenced," she said emotionlessly. "We have lovely beaches for sunbathing."

"Good," and he forced a smile. "What is it—a light or something, or what?"

"A radio signal—to reach the submarine?"

"Yes, to reach the submarine."

"I was unable to bring the radio signal," she mentioned, almost—Frost thought—in passing.

"Oh," the one-eyed man nodded. "So we came all this way and we can't contact the submarine."

"You are resourceful. There are many fishing boats, and the fishing fleet uses radio to coordinate the working of the catch. You can steal a radio."

"Didn't you say something about a boat to take us—"

"Out to the submarine? Yes, but do you see a boat? For three days the boat was to be grounded here with engine trouble. The three days ended yesterday."

"Who owned the boat?" Frost asked.

"That was on a need-to-know basis. I did not need to know. I was not told the name. We have been counted as dead by now."

"Oh," Frost nodded.

"So, you steal a boat and a radio—we call the submarine and maybe it is still there."

"What if it isn't?" Frost asked her.

"Then we try for the Finnish coastline. That is our only hope. If not, then perhaps we blow up a naval installation—there is one nearby. That would at least be a glorious way to—" She grabbed at her head, then screamed, falling to her knees.

Frost dropped down beside her. "What is it?"

"My head!" she screamed, falling into his arms. "My head!"

The one-eyed man clamped his gloved left hand over her mouth, stifling the scream.

He now knew what had been wrong. All along. . . .

He had abandoned the truck, hoping it would eventually be returned to the old woman and her husband. He remembered, ashamed, he had not even asked the woman's name. He had abandoned the two AKMs as well; traveling with them on foot was useless and betraying. Who walks the streets of any major city carrying an assault rifle?

He abandoned the truck within a half mile of the Coastal Watch facility of Kubasov Naval Centre. With the girl beside him, tears streaming down her face with the pain she endured, he walked now toward it, seeing the bright lights from the sentry towers.

"This is suicide—suicide," she told him.

"I know—don't worry about it," Frost answered. Earlier, after the first spasms of pain had brought her to her knees beside him, and he had calmed her finally, he had left her with the truck, inspecting the dock area. There were police everywhere, he assumed watching for him.

That the Russians would not expect someone to attempt the impossible—the penetration of a naval facility—was all he counted on.

He had gotten through his entire life on brashness, daring, stubbornness. He was too old, he realized, to change that now. He would approach the guard station, then simply murder the guard—quietly if possible, noisily if not. He would hotwire the first available vehicle and drive it toward the docks, shoot his way through and steal a patrol boat. He had hatched what he optimistically called "the plan" earlier when vainly looking for a way to steal a boat from the docks. He had seen the power boats with which the Navy patrolled the harbor.

It was the only chance. Assuming an anti-Soviet underground existed in Riga as it did in Moscow, to find it would have been next to impossible, and he doubted they used a radio. With radio signal monitoring equipment such as it was, it would have been their doom.

He stopped at the end of the street, staring toward the naval facility. "You will be—"

"Killed," Frost said soullessly. "You told me that. I'm dead already here. Life is out there. I can't see how you or anybody else could live in a place like this. A gun is a dangerous subversive tool, speaking one's own mind is evil, thinking is dangerous. No—dead is meaningless. If I get out of here, I'll have a life to lose again. Only then. There's nothing to lose now. Nothing."

As the one-eyed man started toward the gates, he

almost wished that Bess were there. What he'd said had been so profound, she could have written it down for posterity.

He listened to his own heels clicking on the shoveled and plowed roadway, the pavement almost dry, his breath coming in huge billowing clouds, He wondered how one said, "Die you Commie S.O.B." in Russian. He mentally and physically shrugged. He was sure when he killed the man, the man would somehow sense it.

Frost waited until a vehicle crossed between the guard posts, so the chainlink fence would be opened. He increased his pace, to reach the gate before it closed.

Five yards from the gate, the nearer of the two visible guards shouted something in Russian. Frost didn't even try to understand it. Instead, from where it had been awkwardly stuffed up the sleeve of his heavy woolen coat, he withdrew one of the two Smith & Wesson revolvers. Aiming with one hand like a duelist, the hammer cocked back under his thumb, he squeezed the trigger.

"Die!" He pulled the trigger back. The .38 bucked in his hand. The nearer of the two guards suddenly had a third eye in the middle of his forehead.

Frost swung the muzzle of the revolver, the second guard's movement almost in slow motion as the muzzle of Frost's revolver settled. The AKM the guard held was coming up. Frost fired, once, then again—a blotch of red in the neck, a second appearing in the guard's right cheek. The AKM discharged into the pavement.

The one-eyed man paused for an instant, letting the revolver hang limply at his right side.

"Arika, come!" he shouted. Then he started to run, stopping beside the nearer of the two guards, snatching at the man's AKM, catching it up in his left hand, pocketing the Smith revolver, then snatching the bayonet from the sheath on the man's belt.

The magazines stolen from the earlier AKMs were tucked inside his belt, five of them, and Frost didn't bother with any more. No time for it. Arika had another five more.

Frost ran to the second guard, the eyes wide open in death. He reached down and snatched up the second assault rifle.

"Arika," he snarled.

Already a siren sounded across the base, and in the distance he could see headlights coming toward the gate.

"Arika!"

He looked behind him as he ran toward a pickup-sized truck near the guard post. Arika was walking—slowly.

"Shit!"

Frost reached the truck, a man's face appearing from inside the door, an AKM firing into the night. The one-eyed man hit the pavement and rolled hard left, firing one of the AKM's, the second on the pavement beside him. He heard the shattering glass, heard an answering bark from the man in the car, then nothing.

Frost pushed to his feet, catching up the second AKM, the first held in an assault position by his right hip.

Ten steps to the truck. Was the man still alive? Nine. Eight. He thought he caught a movement. Seven. Frost fired his AKM. The door of the truck spilled outward, a body tumbling down to the pavement, the neck bent at a crazy angle, the face splotched in three places with blood.

Frost stopped. He reached down and grabbed up the third AKM, tossing two onto the seat.

Arika. He looked behind him. She was through the gates, still walking like a toy robot gotten for Christmas with the battery almost gone.

His teeth—he could feel them grit. "Arika!"

He tossed the third assault rifle on the seat, seeing

the lights ahead of them.

"Yes," she answered, still ten yards back.

He had wanted her to drive, so he could shoot.

"Shit," he rasped, running toward her, grabbing her, shaking her. She didn't respond.

Frost's right fist snaked out, the knuckles catching at the tip of her jaw, her body going limp under his hands as he picked her up, carrying her like a child in his arms. Awkwardly, he slid her into the front seat, then across it, then down onto the floor.

She had given him the frequency for the submarine, just in case. "Just in case," he snarled. He turned the key in the ignition. Both pistols stuffed into his trouser belt, an AKM across his lap with the stick changed, two more—he changed those as well—beside him, he let out the clutch. The truck didn't move.

He shrugged, then released the brake.

"Eat it!" he shouted, throwing the stick from first into second as the truck rolled forward, gathering momentum. In the distance, nearing him, he could see lights. He stuck one of the AKMs out the window in his left hand, then opened fire. One headlight out, still another and another. He kept driving.

The remaining headlights grew in size. He fired again. Another two headlights out, but many more still coming, like a wedge formation, coming at him, nearer and nearer.

"Die!" he shouted, wanting them to, suddenly so badly he could taste it. He could taste it because he could smell the sea. It was so near—he had to make it.

"Die! Die!" He pumped the trigger on the AKM, the gun coming up empty. He let it fall from his fist to the pavement—he had two more.

Only the centermost of the headlights remained intact, and as he neared the vehicles, he could see the rest of the wedge—its sides—breaking off. In the middle of the wedge was something massive, its gray outlining looming up like a ghost in a nightmare.

"Holy shit—" It was an amphibious landing vehicle, armored. A machinegun opened up near the top of its outline in the night.

The windshield in front of Frost shattered as he ducked.

He cut the wheel of the pickup hard right, across a spot of ground that in summer might have had grass, but now had slushy gray snow.

The truck bounced, lurched, and ahead of him was a building that had to be a barracks—no one built buildings that looked like that that weren't barracks halls. He cut the wheel left, the machinegun still firing, a sidewalk between the barracks ahead of him and another to the left looming up, the sidewalk half covered with snow. Frost stomped the clutch, aiming toward the sidewalk.

In the sideview mirror he could see the amphibious craft. It would be no match for the truck in speed, but if it got set up, its machinegun could—"Oh wonderful," he groaned. The amphibious craft stopped in the center of the sidewalk between the barracks halls, the machinegun firing tracer rounds visible in the night.

The one-eyed man glanced from right to left, seeing only narrow walkways between the barracks halls—too narrow.

The glass behind his head shattered, the instrumentation on the dashboard shattering as well, bullets making pinging noises as they ricocheted off the truck body.

There was no choice—he cut the wheel hard left, still aiming he hoped toward the docks, between two of the barracks halls.

He reached down, grabbing the unconscious Arika by the collar of her coat, hauling her closer to him, away from the passenger-side door.

The barracks walls were closing in as Frost aimed the

pickup down the center of the walkway. He could hear it before he could feel it—the twisting and tearing sound of the metal. Then he felt the trembling, the shivering of the truck as the fenders began to peel away, the fenders rising now along the sides of the truck, chips and blade-sized splinters of wood spraying into the air as the truck's forward motion sheared away the siding of the barracks buildings.

At the end of the narrow walkway as the truck groaned ahead, he could see men forming, assault rifles in their hands, the rifles opening up, the windshield in front of him shattering more, glass spraying across the dashboard and the front seat. With his right hand, he covered the girl's eyes.

He could hear the gunfire as it smashed into the truck body, knowing they would be firing for the radiator. And he could see steam rising from it, feel a loss of power in the truck, hear an impossibly loud knocking sound.

He reached the end of the walkway, keeping his foot hard on the gas as he negotiated the turn.

There was a loud popping sound—not gunfire, but the sound of a tire bursting. One of the fenders had apparently broken into a jagged edge. He started skidding right—the left tire, he guessed. Gunfire hammered at him from the assault rifle-armed seamen to his left and behind him.

He fought the wheel, turning into the skid, then turning out of it as the pickup's nose impacted against the side of the barracks hall to his right, peeling away a large section of siding, throwing it into the air, smaller chunks flying through the windshield. The one-eyed man dodged, ducking, still fighting the wheel, most of his steering gone.

The truck bounced, jarred, and there was the clanging sound, unmistakeable as the sound of riding the rim. The car sagged left, and Frost could feel the power going as he stomped harder on the gas, downshifting, but keeping his foot on the gas all the time.

Ahead of him were the lights from the docks. He could see the masts or whatever they were called—he didn't know—of the power boats used by the harbor patrol.

Gunfire continued—behind him, to his left. He glanced left once, two men running up alongside the truck. He wrenched one of the revolvers free of his beltline with his left hand, his right fist locking onto the steering wheel.

The one-eyed man punched the revolver out the window, looking hard left for an instant, pumping the revolver's double-action trigger twice, the nearer of the two men falling away. There was a burst of automatic weapons fire, the vent window and the sideview mirror shattering. Frost's left forearm ached badly. A bullet wound.

But he could still hold the gun.

He fired, twice more, then twice again, the second pursuer dropping, spinning out to the pavement as a bloodied hand reached for the truck body. Frost dropped the revolver out the window, no use for it now.

Fifty yards away was the dock, massive cruisers visible there as well as the patrol boats. He almost prayed they couldn't be started up fast. He couldn't outrun one.

Men—the Russian equivalent of Shore Patrol—blocked the access drive ahead of him.

Frost tucked down, driving the truck straight toward them, bullets whizzing above his head, higher pitched than the whining of the engine, ricochets tearing into the fabric of the seat behind him, tearing at his clothes. He winced once as he felt a slug hit his right forearm.

There was a scream, then another and another, the gunfire ahead of him ceasing as he looked up. The engine was smoking badly and he could smell fire if not see it. The Shore Patrol officers were behind him now, at least two of them still able to stand, running as he glanced back.

There was a patrol boat less than a dozen yards ahead now on the dock and Frost aimed the truck as best he could straight toward it, a man appearing on the deck, an AKM in his hands.

Frost snatched the second revolver, punching it through the space where there had been a windshield, firing once, then again, the rifleman's body twisting, falling.

Frost wrenched up on the emergency brake, stomping the brakes with his right foot, not worrying about the clutch.

He could hear Arika stirring, moaning, as he reached for her, grabbing her and hauling her bodily across the front seat and out on the driver's side. He stood her up, then bent into her, letting her fall across his left shoulder. He reached back into the truck cab for the two AKMs, finding them, shifting one into his bloodied left hand, the other in his right, the safety off, welded to his right hip in one-handed assault position.

Two of the Shore Patrolmen were still coming. Frost opened up, the two men slowing their run, firing. Frost felt something tearing at his left leg, a wild, sudden, burning sensation of pain in his left thigh. He kept firing, then the second of the Shore Patrolmen going down.

Limping, his left leg screaming at him not to move, he moved on, toward the patrol boat.

He dropped one of the AKMs, shouldering the semiconscious girl from the dock onto the deck of the patrol boat. He snatched up the AKM, turning, firing a long burst toward the vehicles storming toward him—a useless burst. They were too far away for one-handed hip shooting.

He threw the emptied AKM onto the deck, then hauled himself up over the rope railing and off the dock, onto the deck.

There was a deck gun—a machinegun. He pulled the tarp from it, not recalling the make or model, but sensing innately the mechanics of how it worked. There was a large "magazine" in place and Frost worked back the machinegun's bolt, loosening the bolts holding it locked down, then turning the muzzle toward the end of the street.

"Eat lead, suckers," he snarled, starting to pump the trigger. It shot high and he lowered the muzzle, popping out one set of headlights, then a second.

He heard something—but that was impossible. He felt it. He wheeled, letting loose of the machinegun, a man with a knife coming for him from behind, perhaps a sleeping crewman.

Frost sidestepped, falling against the machinegun, then slumping to the deck. The man lunged, Frost rolled and punched upward with the bayonet he'd stolen from one of the guards at the gate.

There was a guttural belching sound as the man with the knife seemed to stop, then fell forward. Frost rolled away.

The man was dead.

Frost pushed himself to his feet, Arika stirring on the deck. "Get up—wake up!" She didn't.

"Hell!" he rasped, starting down into what he called the cockpit—he was never good with nautical terms. "Pilot's cabin?" he mused aloud.

He found the key, turned it, and saw what looked like a starter button. He pulled out what looked like a hand choke, then whispered, almost praying, "Please start—please."

The engines beneath him rumbled, but didn't catch. He let in the choke slightly, glancing around the side of the exposed cabin, seeing more vehicles coming, and running men with guns. "Please," he almost begged, punching the starter again. The engines rumbling, starting to catch, Frost played with the choke. The engines then fired fully to life.

"All right!"

He moved forward, limping badly now on his right leg, his trouser leg soaked with blood.

He reached down, to the chest of the dead man, wrenching out the bayonet, then hacked with it at the mooring lines to the dock.

He had the forward line, then limped aft, to catch the aft line.

A burst of automatic weapons fire hammered into the deck and Frost fell back.

"Bite it," he snarled, limping forward to the machinegun on the deck. He snatched at the big weapon, wheeling it around, firing a long ragged line across the street, toward the running men who'd opened up on him. Then he turned the gun all the way aft, firing, a long, vertical burst severing the aft mooring line.

"Ha!" He exulted in it. He laughed—he felt he was going crazy.

"Arika, wake up, dammit!"

He lurched against the controls, found what looked like the selector, and put it into what he hoped was reverse, the bow lurching into the dock. He moved the selector, the boat shuddering under him, then backing up.

"Arika—find that frequency before they jam us!"

The girl moved on the deck. He could see her as he twisted the steering wheel—it looked like a steering wheel, acted like a steering wheel. "The hell with nautical terms," he snapped to himself. He moved the selector into what he hoped was a forward speed. The boat surged ahead suddenly, sideswiping a boat moored near it, and there was a groaning sound as the boats separated. Frost worked the wheel back and forth, jockeying away, then pulled hard left and toward the mouth of the harbor.

Machinegun fire was ripping down on him from a cutter as he passed it. The one-eyed man ducked, shouting, "Arika—get on that deck gun!"

The instruments were shattering, the glass in front of him cracking. "Arika!"

He swore he'd throw her overboard.

Suddenly he could hear it—the answering sound of the deck gun. He glanced forward. The woman was behind the machinegun, firing up at the cutter, the cutter's fire suddenly still. A body fell with a splashing sound, loudly audible.

Frost fumbled with the selector, searching for a higher speed, finding it, the patrol boat shooting ahead under him, his body thrown back with the motion. He glanced forward once more—Arika was still at the deck gun, standing beside it limply, shaking.

"Arika, find that frequency for the sub. Come on, kid—you can do it!"

She was starting aft toward the pilot's cabin. Frost hoped the radio hadn't been shot up.

She walked past him and, in a second he could see her searching the cabin, finding what at least looked to him like a radio. "This is it," she called out.

"Get the frequency."

"Wait a minute—yes." He glanced toward her. "Emigre calling Daddy. Emigre calling Daddy. Call me home, over."

Frost stared at the radio, forgetting the approaching mouth of the harbor, forgetting the boats already assembling there to block his escape. "Emigre calling Daddy. Call me home, over."

Nothing came back on the radio.

Chapter Eighteen

Frost looked away from the radio, feeling the insane desire to cry aloud. He didn't. He barked to Arika. "Get at the controls here—I'll get the deck gun."

"But your leg," she said, staring at him. "Your hands."

"Better dead than red, kid." And he grabbed her left hand and balled her fist on the wheel.

He started limping forward, snatching up one of the AKMs, changing sticks in it.

"Look around and see if there's another magazine for this deck gun—should be out almost. And then give it all the speed you've got and go right through 'em like threadin' a needle."

He dropped awkwardly to his right knee, his left leg screaming at him not to. He shouldered the AKM—the distance was three hundred yards or so. He started firing—he had ammo to burn. He took as his target a knot of dark figures on the deck of a patrol boat, identical to the one he had stolen, moving into the center of the harbor.

He started firing. He blinked—a brilliant, blinding spotlight came on, aimed at him. Squinting against the light, he fired a long, ragged burst, then another. The second burst did the work, the light blowing out.

"A magazine, Hank!"

Frost pushed himself to his feet, shouldering the AKM on its sling cross-body behind his back, muzzle down.

He limped back, getting the magazine. It weighed a good thirty pounds, he judged. Carrying it in both hands, he limped forward, shouting to her, "Stay on that radio—they gotta be out there." To himself, he whispered it again. "They gotta be out there."

He found the magazine release latch on the machinegun, then turned the machinegun toward the cutters and patrol boats starting to block the harbor mouth. He fired the big weapon in long bursts toward the center of the harbor mouth, to keep the ships away.

The magazine was empty and he worked the release, then inserted the fresh one, more easily because he'd found the release first. He worked the bolt, then turned the deck gun, leaning his weight against it. His left leg would no longer support him.

"Keep on that radio," he shouted once more, then started firing. A hundred yards now and the gap at the mouth of the harbor was closing as Frost aimed the deck gun toward the nearest ship. Above him, he heard the whirring of helicopter rotor blades. "I needed that," he rasped, ceasing to fire the deck gun, snatching at the AKM. A burst of machinegun fire ripped into the deck beside him from above. He dropped to his knees, the pain in the left leg almost making him pass out.

But he shouldered the AKM, leveling it at the helicopter, turning now for another pass.

He started firing, telling himself to ignore the machinegun fire ripping toward him across the bow, across the deck. Chips of wood and paint sprayed against his face and hands.

He felt it then—before he actually remembered seeing it—a shuddering, then he saw a burst of brilliant yellow and black flame. A fireball exploded, hot metal and fabric raining down on him as the helicopter seemed to vaporize.

His hands over his face, the AKM dropped now, he crawled back toward the deck gun, reaching up to it, the gun swaying under his weight against its mounts. He got to a standing position, them aimed the deck gun. A patrol boat, its identical deck gun firing, was closing the escape route at the mouth of the harbor.

"A duel, huh," he smiled to the anonymous deck gunner on the other patrol boat.

He leveled the machinegun, firing short bursts, feeling wood and bits of lead splattering toward him as the deck around him seemed to explode under the opposing gunfire.

He kept shooting, shooting, one burst after another, his eye glued to the sight.

He had lost track of the number of rounds, then experienced a sick feeling as the bolt clicked on an empty chamber.

Twenty-five yards to go now. Frost stared—helpless for the moment—toward the opposing deck gunner. He could see the body as it fell.

Frost sagged to the deck—what was left of it—finding one of the AKMs. He shook it to get rid of the debris which had half covered it, then rammed a fresh stick up the well, turning it toward the nearer of the ships.

They were even with it, the deck gun opening up, missing by a wide margin.

Frost shouldered the AKM. He didn't miss. A long burst cut into the new deck gunner, dropping him.

He looked away for an instant—ahead was the open sea. "Give it all the gas you can," he shouted. He started aft, toward the pilot's cabin, toward Arika and the radio.

He slumped down the steps, stumbling, then pulled

himself up beside her.

"You're dying," she gasped, looking at him.

"And you're so fuckin' cheerful." He took the wheel from her hands, pushing her aside. "Work the radio—keep it up. Don't stop or I'll throw you overboard—now."

The one-eyed man looked behind them. Patrol boats—at least one cutter—were all coming, and in the sky behind them he could make out the lights of another helicopter. He hoped it wasn't a gunship.

He closed his eye for an instant, sagging against the controls, a wave of nausea passing over him. She was right, he thought—maybe he was dying. Loss of blood was heavy.

He didn't remember how far out the Soviets claimed their territorial limits—but if by some miracle the sub was there, it would be outside that limit. He turned the wheel right, aiming straight out to sea.

"We'll never make it," the woman was saying.

"Shut up except for workin' the damn radio, Arika. Or so help me I'll—" He shook his head to clear it, then heard her voice: "Emigre calling Daddy."

"Daddy! Where the hell are ya!" Frost screamed into the icy wind.

There was no answer.

Chapter Nineteen

Frost snatched the microphone from her, hitting the push-to-talk button. Three cutters were closing fast and with the gauges shot out on the dashboard, he had no way of telling if he had yet reached the territorial limit. He didn't even know what the territorial limit was for the Soviet Union.

"Emigre calling Daddy. Mayday dammit. Mayday. Emigre calling Daddy—bring us home!" He stared at the microphone, glared at it, then pushed the button again. "Over!"

There was static, crackling, "What's the matter, Ace—got the Commies on your ass? Over."

Frost almost screamed. He was hallucinating—he knew he had to be.

"Daddy, this is Emigre. Come back with that again, over."

"You call me Daddy one more time, Frost, and I'll bend the barrel of my .44 over your head. Over."

"O'Hara?"

"Right here with Uncle Sam and the cavalry—er, Navy—you know. Keep coming, sport. We got you on radar."

"Mike?"

"Yeah—over, already."

Frost threw down the microphone, laughing.

"What is the matter, Hank?" the woman beside him asked.

"Not a damn thing, kid." Frost let the engines out the extra few R.P.M.s they had, looking over his shoulder, shouting at the Soviet cutters as they closed, "Go to hell!"

"Daddy, this is Emigre. How soon to contact? Got a bunch of S.O.B.'s on my butt—over."

"Keep her coming, sport—keep her comin' make it a nautical mile they tell me. Can't touch ya' till then. Keep humpin'—over."

"Emigre out." Frost threw down the microphone.

He turned to the girl. "Get one of the AKMs. Start shootin' at those cutters as soon as they open up."

"They are faster—they have deck guns."

"That was my best friend, kid—all we gotta do is drive and we're home. Just shut up and do as I say!" Spray washed across the bow as Frost's boat plowed through the waves, the spray washing against his face and clothes, icy cold, the engines throbbing beneath him.

The girl screamed. "A helicopter!"

"Oh shit," Frost snarled, glancing behind him, then staring ahead again, refusing to look at it for an instant. "So close—so damn close!" He turned to the woman. "Take the wheel. Steer a straight course just like we're going. Keep the radio open. I'm taking some pot shots at that chopper."

"But a nautical mile—we'll never—"

"Shut up!" Frost finally lost it, he realized after he did it. His right hand had shot out, the back of it crashing down across her right cheek, knocking her to the deck. "I don't know what the hell crazy thing they did to you—but I'll lay every dime I got they put one of those damned electrodes into your head and you don't know your own mind. Now, drive this damned thing or I'll shoot you and throw you overboard and drive myself—now!"

The woman's eyes were glassy, her left hand rubbing her cheek. She said nothing, but took the wheel.

Frost stumbled back toward the AKM propped in the corner of the pilot's cabin or wheel house or whatever it was called.

He worked the bolt on the AKM, shouldering the rifle, the muzzle weaving, half from the motion of the patrol boat under him, half from his own weakness. "Damn!" he snarled, settling the front sight, getting the line-up, then opening fire on the bubble dome of the pursuit helicopter.

He missed; or if he hit, could see no effect.

"I see a periscope—no—a conning tower!"

Frost looked behind him, then past the girl and at the open sea. He saw it too.

He shouldered the AKM, firing, the rifle jamming. As he fought to clear it. "Emigre, this is Daddy. You're home—don't shoot any more—over!"

The helicopter was turning back.

Frost dropped the rifle and sank to his knees, throwing down the rifle.

It was over. The cutters pulled back as well, rolling now with the waves as their speed slowed.

"Frost!"

The one-eyed man looked up, out to sea. The submarine was close. "Cut your engines—cut 'em!" the same voice, not Mike O'Hara's, shouted over a bullhorn.

"Cut the engines—dead!" Frost shouted to Arika.

He heard them cut out, then closed his eye.

He could feel the motion, hear the bullhorn getting louder and louder as they drifted. Then he heard the voice without the bullhorn.

"Are you all right, Captain Frost?"

Frost looked up, seeing an American face—apple pie, motherhood and baseball written all over it—with a big smile.

Frost heard himself laugh—he was passing out. He called up to the deck of the nuclear submarine, "You tell Mike O'Hara that if I were gay, I'd kiss him!" He was very tired, and he fell over. . . .

"Boy—you're lucky you got shot up or I'd punch you out," O'Hara laughed, then put his hand on Frost's left shoulder.

"Somehow—" the one-eyed man nodded, feeling nausea from the pain killers and the anesthesia—"I should have known you'd be here waiting for me."

"You know how many strings I hadda pull for an FBI agent to get shipped out on a nuke sub? And I hate the water."

"How is Bess?"

"She made me go. You didn't get home that day after they snatched you, the silly woman was on the horn to me. She loves you, Frost—hell if I understand it. Anyway, soon as they got you and that Russian dame on board and I knew you were still mostly in one piece, I got 'em to get out a radio message."

"They use lasers," Frost corrected him.

"Yeah—well, she knows you're alive and okay—mostly anyway."

"Friend—it's a good word," Frost smiled.

"Yeah, well don't go gettin' sentimental."

"Friend." Frost extended his right hand, O'Hara taking it in his.

"Friend," O'Hara nodded.

"Did they check her?"

"That electrode stuff you were mumblin' about—

somethin' in her head?"

"Yeah, she's got one."

"I don't know what it is you think she's got, sport—but much more than bullet wounds and appendicitis, these Navy docs can't do. You want somebody lookin' in her head—or yours—you gotta wait."

"Mike, she's not real. She's—maybe like a machine, like a time bomb."

"Hey," O'Hara's voice softened. "Hank, ya had a hard time. Just relax."

"No—don't take your eyes off her. And don't hurt her. It's not her, but what they did to her. That's what I hadda tell ya—their defectors. They've got them controlled with these electrodes, and they can manipulate their behavior."

"It's them sci-fi books you read, Frost. I always tell ya, read Westerns. They're wholesome stuff, not this gobbledy gook monster crap."

"Listen." The one-eyed man felt himself going, the drugs getting to him. "Promise—watch her."

O'Hara nodded. "A dame that looks like that—yeah. I'll watch her. Sure."

The last thing Frost heard was O'Hara saying, "You rest, buddy." And for once, Hank Frost decided he'd take Mike O'Hara's advice. He closed his eye.

Chapter Twenty

His right arm was stiff. His left arm hurt too, and he felt stupid using the cane to help his left leg. The cane had been fluoroscoped as he'd entered—Frost guessed perhaps they'd been looking for a sword or something in it. Maybe booze, but he doubted a fluoroscope would show that.

He'd left O'Hara at the front steps, the two men promising each other to get together for dinner that night.

He sat now in the office of CIA Section Chief for Eastern European Affairs. He sat alone, studying the tip of the cane, looking through the pale gray-colored open venetian blinds at the grass patch between the building and one of the parking lots. He wanted it over with, done. There was Bess to get back to—they'd spoken on the telephone but hadn't seen each other yet. There was dinner that night with Mike O'Hara.

There was life to resume.

"Captain Frost—no, don't get up."

Frost had started to rise as the tall, beanpole-thin man had entered the room—not to rise out of politeness, but out of stiffness.

"I'm Halsey Burns," the man said with a smile, extending his right hand. Frost stayed seated, taking the handshake. It was professionally firm, very dry and warm. The man's hair caught Frost's eye—it was a dark, almost unnatural gunmetal gray, neatly combed and cut short in the Ivy League style of the 1950s.

"You've had quite an ordeal, Captain. I hope your wounds aren't too painful."

"I've hurt worse," Frost nodded, finding a Camel in the half empty pack in his pocket as Burns walked around the desk, then opened a top drawer. Frost started frisking himself for a book of matches, then looked up. Burns' right hand extended across the desk, a lighter in it. As Frost leaned into the flame, he said through a mouthful of smoke, "That's my lighter."

"Yes," and Burns closed it, then set it down at the edge of the desk, just in front of where Frost sat.

"This is yours, too," and he reached into the drawer, producing Frost's Rolex Sea Dweller. "And these." He handed across Frost's wallet, money clip and keys.

Frost took the watch, studied it a moment. It was running, and according to the digital clock on the window ledge behind Burns' desk, in perfect time.

"We took the liberty of setting it for you. Had Rolex give it a good cleaning, too—just a little courtesy."

"And a way of checking it out?"

Burns only smiled, then said, "You spoke to the FBI agent—er, Mr.—"

"O'Hara," Frost nodded.

"Something about electrodes? In the brain?"

"Have you checked Arika Gorki?"

"As a matter of fact we have. It didn't show up immediately, but we found a small scar not far from—well, you wouldn't be interested in the medical details. Our Miss Gorki agreed to surgery and we discovered there was a foreign object—"

"Very foreign," Frost smiled.

Burns didn't. "A foreign object. It was near the cerebral cortex. It was removed. Miss Gorki is recovering nicely. I'll confess, though, our own research people and outside people we've engaged haven't been able to decipher the object's exact nature. Perhaps you can help us."

"You checked me, I assume—when I was in the hospital here the first day I arrived."

"Yes, we found nothing abnormal. But we did with Miss Gorki. What is it supposed to be, Captain Frost?"

"The doctor in charge of the hospital where I was held—he detailed to me, to at least some extent. It is a KGB project. Supposedly, that's why they grabbed me. They were trying to solve the problem of political and ideological defections. They wanted a way to control what they considered subversive elements."

"Why would they want you? You're certainly not a Soviet dissident."

"Let me finish—and like I say, I'm just repeating pretty much what the doctor told me as best I can remember it. But they wanted to control these people, anyway, so they implanted some kind of electrode or something in their brains and could use laser transmissions to activate the electrode and control the subject. He mentioned some ballerina—"

"We're looking into that."

"I got the impression they'd done it to a lot of people. Then they hit on the idea of taking certain Americans and doing the same thing. People they could turn on, like death machines or something, with this electrode at some future date. Like with the ballerina—they said maybe if she were performing at some sensitive function, well—they could make her kill."

"What caused you to consider Miss Gorki had been given one of these electrodes?"

Frost stubbed out his cigarette in the ashtray on the

desk in front of him. "I kept having a feeling about her—that something was wrong. I couldn't put my finger on it though until we actually started out along the escape route. It was her behavior—erratic. I'll give her credit. She complained about these terrible headaches. I think—maybe subconsciously on her part—she was fighting the messages sent by the electrode. One minute she'd be up, the next minute down, emotionally. One minute courageous, the next cowardly. Somehow, I figured maybe they got wind of her working as a contract employee for you guys, nabbed her and—"

"She was hospitalized with appendicitis for a short period. But we had no idea that—"

"I guess that was the idea," Frost nodded. "So you'd have no idea. She could have been poisoned or something to fake the appendicitis. Whatever."

"Captain Frost, I'd like to ask a favor. Your country would like to ask the favor, actually."

"Go back to Russia, right? You're nuts."

Burns laughed—too heartily, Frost thought. "No—hardly that. No. Much simpler and totally painless. In fact, it should prove positively therapeutic. I'd like you voluntarily to submit to hypnotism, and under the hypnotic suggestion you can probably recall details that have eluded your conscious memory, or in fact things your conscious memory may have rejected. Not just about the electrodes, but the whole escape from the Soviet Union. You have seen things most Americans, even American agents, don't get to see. Like that farm you mentioned to Agent O'Hara—where the woman helped you. What amount of acreage did it appear to use in cultivation? Little details like that that have nothing to do with the electrode business, or your experiences really, but incidental bits and pieces of intelligence."

"And more detailed recollection of what that doctor

told me?"

Burns only nodded.

"What guarantee do I have you won't try something funny—like giving a post-hypnotic suggestion that I forget all this? Something like that?"

"I think you have the best guarantee we could give—albeit unintentional. You spoke extensively with Agent O'Hara while aboard the submarine. The FBI would never allow us to debrief one of their agents without another of their people present. So we couldn't blot out Agent O'Hara's memory, could we? As long as he knows, it would be meaningless to cause you to forget." Then Burns took a long, slender cigar from a box on his desk, the box looking to be made of stone with carvings on the lid.

He rolled the cigar in the tips of his fingers.

"What?" Frost asked.

Burns took a small object from the pocket of his vest—it looked like a coin the size of a silver dollar. He thumbnailed open something at the edge, revealing a little guillotine-like device. He clipped the tip of the cigar with it, not yet putting the cigar in his mouth. "I'll ask that you mention your experiences to no one else besides Agent O'Hara—since as far as he is concerned, we really have no choice. Especially that journalist friend of yours, Miss Stallman."

"Nuts," Frost smiled.

"She is a journalist!"

"Still nuts," Frost reiterated. "What I tell her privately stays private. The only way she'd put any of this in print is if you guys started playing it funny with me. And that's something you'd better keep in mind."

"I fail to see," Burns nodded, lighting the cigar finally—Frost pegged the lighter as a Dunhill—"what this obsession is with 'blowing the whistle' so to speak on American Intelligence procedures."

"I don't have an obsession—I just like insurance. Wouldn't drive my car without it, wouldn't live in my apartment without renter's insurance—you know. Had a house—man, first thing I'd buy is fire insurance. It's like carrying a gun. Most of the time you don't need it, but it's sure damned nice to have it around when ya do, right?"

Burns smiled. "I get your point." He cleared his throat, then coughed loudly, looking at the cigar as if it smelled bad. It did, Frost thought. "But you'll submit to hypnosis?"

The one-eyed man swallowed hard. He only nodded. . . .

"So they didn't tell ya a thing?" O'Hara asked.

Frost just shook his head.

"Well, here's to ignorance," and O'Hara raised his glass of straight Myers's dark rum.

Frost felt himself smiling, then raised his glass of Seagrams and ice, clinking it against O'Hara's. "Where you goin' now?" O'Hara asked him.

"Quietly insane—maybe not so quietly. I'll see." Then, shrugging, Frost went on, "Goin' back to Bess—pick up on seven weeks of my life. Find myself a new High Power. Mine never did turn up."

"Probably one of them KGB creeps has got it—maybe they gave it to old Andropov himself. You know—have a nice regime, Yuri. Start it off with a bang."

Frost laughed. "That old lady at that farm—she was a Communist more or less. But she helped me out. Saved my life really."

"Yeah, well," O'Hara stammered. "One good apple don't make the rest of the barrel quit bein' rotten, ya know."

"How can I refute logic like that?" Frost laughed, downing more of his drink. Then he looked at O'Hara, saying, "You think that electrode stuff is for real?"

"Well, they found one in that Russian dame's head, you said. What's her name?"

"Arika Gorki."

"Yeah—Gorki. I dunno. Here—" and O'Hara reached under his coat, almost as if he were pulling a gun. When his hand emerged, there was a small box in it, gift wrapped in foil.

"Look, Mike, I'm already engaged," Frost laughed.

"Shut up and just take the present, will ya—here," and O'Hara shoved the box across the table and looked away.

Frost picked up the box, then opened the foil wrapping. It was secured with transparent tape and Frost used his table knife to cut the tape. He spilled the box inside the wrapping out onto the tablecloth. He looked up, the waitress coming to the table.

"Would either of you gentlemen care for dessert?"

"You got apple pie?" O'Hara asked.

"Sure—how about some ice cream—"

"Yeah, but put the cheese on first, then the ice cream over it. And just plain vanilla—nothin' with nuts in it."

"Yes, sir," the woman smiled. She was pretty, Frost noticed as she looked at him, "And you, sir?"

"Same—without the cheese, please," Frost nodded.

Frost and O'Hara both ordered coffee as well, and the woman left. The one-eyed man looked at the box, not opening it.

"Open it, will ya," O'Hara snapped.

Frost laughed, then opened the box. Inside was a green leather sheath and a green-handled knife. "You know how hard it was to find an original Gerber MkI? Before they made the handle black?"

The one-eyed man removed the knife from the sheath,

feeling it in his hand. The feel was there, the feel he liked. "Thank you," Frost said. He wasn't going to tell O'Hara he had three of them put away for a rainy day, because this one would be special. "Thank you, my friend."

Chapter Twenty-one

Frost stopped leaning on the cane as he walked, still limping, down the passenger ramp from the 747, then into the gate. Just beyond the gate, in the corridor, he saw the face he'd longed to see all the weeks in Russia. He saw Bess.

He walked toward her, seeing her eyes fill with tears. Her arms outstretched to him, she started to run, coming into his arms—almost knocking him over. "Thank God," she whispered hoarsely.

The one-eyed man pushed her back a bit, so he could look at her. "Do I look all right—what's the matter?" she asked, trying to smile.

"You look all right—more than that," he told her, folding her into his arms and holding her close against him. He could smell the perfume of her hair and he kissed it.

"I cooked one of your favorites," she called out from the kitchen.

"Macaroni and cheese out of a box?" Frost sang back.

"Shut up," she snapped. "No," and he could hear

her laugh. He sat in the reclining chair, his left leg stiff but no longer really paining him. He could see some of the lights of Atlanta in the distance through the apartment window. It was good to be home—and he smiled, realizing that for the first time ever in his life, he had a home. With his parents divorced as a child, he had lived in military academies, near college campuses, and finally in the jungles and wetlands of Viet Nam. After that, after the loss of his eye, there had been an apartment, but he hadn't really lived there. Then he had taken up mercenary soldiering, and when, like most mercenaries, he'd found there wasn't a steady living in it, he had taken up on and off residence in the apartment in South Bend, Indiana, to be near his occasional employer, Diablo Protective Services. "We fight like the devil for you!"

Then he had met Bess in Africa. Things had never been the same. Even before they had begun living together she had given him an emotional home, a place to run to, a place to trust—herself.

"Okay, what's for dinner?" he shouted over his shoulder, not turning around to look. "I give up."

"Be surprised," he heard her call back, almost defensively.

He shook his head, then worked the side handle on the recliner and moved his weight forward, the footstool portion of the chair folding down. He stood up, stretched his leg, hurting a little as he moved it, then turned and started toward the dining area.

The table was set with candles and a lacy tablecloth. He felt almost civilized.

"What's the occasion?" he called out.

"You're back—you know that," he heard her answer after a moment.

"Oh," and he sat down at the head of the smallish table. He could smell the food but couldn't quite identify it.

"Coming in a minute," she called out.

He closed his eye. The sound he had heard—it hadn't been a kitchen noise. More of a scratching sound. "You didn't get a cat or something while I was gone?" he called out.

"No, why?"

"Nothing," he answered, feeling bad already about lying. But he heard the scratching sound again as he stood up.

He started walking—limping—quickly but evenly toward the bedroom. He had never realized how far a walk it was before. "Stay in the kitchen for a second!" he called out, trying to keep his voice normal sounding.

He opened the closet in the bedroom they shared, and under empty suitcases belonging to Bess, he found the Safariland SWAT bag he so often used as luggage. He quickly—almost frantically—worked the zipper. The Interdynamics KG-99 9mm assault pistol was there, with sling and flash suppressor in place. He reached out one of the thirty-six-round magazines. He breathed a long sigh, relieved for once Bess knew not terribly much about firearms—otherwise she might have thought to unload the magazines to release spring tension.

He rammed the magazine up the well, then snatched up two more loaded spares, ramming them into this belt. He started back toward the dinette area of the apartment. He no longer heard the scratching sound.

"Nerves," he commented to himself. It was probably just a scratching sound—nothing more.

He moved the KG-99's sling onto his left shoulder over his head, keeping the weapon cross-body under his right arm.

"What's the—" Bess was starting out of the kitchen,

a large platter in her pot-holdered hands. "It's hot," she said, just to talk, he thought. Her eyes flashed toward his eye, then following he could see as he turned toward the door. He pointed toward the door with the muzzle of the KG-99.

He looked back at her—there was a sick, tired look in her green eyes.

He gestured toward the kitchen and she set the platter down on a mat on the table, setting the potholders beside it. She undid the strings of the apron around her waist and set it on the back of her chair, then smoothing her skirt along her thighs, she walked back toward the kitchen.

Frost followed her, stopping beside the counter.

"My rice will burn," she said absently.

The one-eyed man turned around to the kitchen stove and found the burner control—he knew at least how to boil water for instant coffee—and shut it off. "It'll still burn," she said, reaching past him, lifting the pot and moving it to another burner.

He heard a noise—this time louder.

"Those locks I had put on really work," he smiled. He extended his right hand, placing it on her right shoulder as she turned her face over her shoulder toward the door. He pushed her down into a deep bend. She dropped to her knees on the floor, behind the counter separating the kitchen from the dinette area.

The one-eyed man glanced down at her once. He could read her eyes. "Not again—not now," they were saying.

He felt his right eyebrow rise by way of answer as his left hand found the bolt knob on the KG-99 and drew it back, slowly, then eased it forward, the bolt closing and stripping out the top round in the magazine.

There was a thud, then a tearing sound of wood and

metal, the door into the hallway splintering and crashing inward. Frost saw faces behind the door—faces he didn't know, but he knew why they were there.

The first finger of his right hand worked the trigger on the KG-99, the gun bucking in his hands as he kept pumping. The first of the four men in the doorway shouted something as he doubled over and dropped, the man behind him firing a shotgun.

The one-eyed man hit the floor beside Bess, the shotgun pellets tearing into the cabinet doors behind him. Another blast followed, the sound deafening in the confined space of the apartment. Bess screamed, her hands held over her ears.

Frost reached the KG-99 up over the counter top, snapping off a fast, two-round semi-automatic burst, then tucking down as gunfire—shotgun and pistol from the sound of it—ripped into the counter top. There was a crashing sound, of glass or china.

"My dinner!" Bess screamed.

"Women!" the one-eyed man snarled, pumping the KG-99 again as he edged it around to his left along the side of the counter.

He heard a groan, assuming he'd wounded someone, but not figuring on a solid hit just potshotting as he was.

Then he heard another sound, one he hadn't heard before in the gunfight—a light caliber submachinegun. Then came a shout, "Federal officers—drop your weapons!"

The one-eyed man—against his better judgment—poked his head over the top of the counter, the KG-99 in an assault position across the counter top. Two of the four men who burst through the doorway into the apartment were down on the floor—at least one, the one Frost had shot first, was obviously dead. The other two had their hands raised, and behind them, in the doorway, were three men, one wearing a three-piece suit, the other two in casual clothes, the one who wore the suit carrying an Uzi submachinegun.

The man with the Uzi called across the room, "Captain Frost, you can rest easy now, I think."

"Who the hell—?" It was Bess, and Frost glanced to his right. She was standing beside him.

"I'm Arnold Liebermann. I'm attached to Air Force Intelligence. Mr. Burns—I believe you know him, Captain Frost."

Frost said to Bess, "The CIA guy I told you about."

"Mr. Burns," Liebermann went on, "asked us to keep an eye on you." He evidently noticed Frost's eyepatch then, saying, "I didn't mean any insult by—"

"Never mind," Frost murmured, searching for a cigarette. He didn't find one.

"Here," and Bess was ripping open a fresh package of Camels, then struck a kitchen match. He watched her as she inhaled, not giving him the cigarette.

"Thanks," he nodded, looking back to Liebermann.

"Mr. Burns assumed the KGB would try—"

"What the hell's this KG shit? Some guy hired us to—" It was one of the two standing gunmen in the doorway.

"KGB," Frost told the man, the man looking across his shoulder, back at Frost now. "It's the Committee for State Security of the Soviet Union."

"Holy—I ain't no fuckin' Commie!"

Liebermann was okay, Frost decided. He said to the would-be killer, "Can't win 'em all."

Frost heard Bess sniffing loudly, then looked at her, following her gaze to the platter on the table. There was a pistol sitting in the middle of it, and the platter was half off the table, the dead man Frost had shot holding the edge of the table cloth in a bloody fist.

"My dinner," she said finally.

Frost set down the KG-99 and put his right arm around her. "Like the man said," he almost whispered, "you can't win 'em all."

She just looked at him, then gave him the butt of the cigarette.

Chapter Twenty-two

They had rented the summer home in the Georgia mountains under the name of Berkeley—Mr. and Mrs. Richard Berkeley of Chicago. It was far out of the city limits of the small town nearby, and behind the house itself was a six-acre partially wooded lot, and at the far end of the lot a rolling embankment of red Georgia clay. Frost hefted his new High Power in his right fist. It was the first time he would shoot it, picking it up just prior to leaving Atlanta under escort of more of the Air Force Intelligence people Burns had gotten to be shepherds.

After Frost had reached Washington, one of the first calls he'd made after talking with Bess had been to his buddy Ron Mahovsky, headman of Metalife Industries in Reno, Pennsylvania. The one-eyed man had needed a new High Power, assuming the one he'd lost when he'd been kidnapped by the KGB would never be recovered. Mahovsky had been round butting a K-Frame Smith in his shop when Frost had called, but agreed to drop everything to fabricate a High Power. "Fabricate" had been the right word. He'd convinced the one-eyed man that the basically stock guns he'd used before weren't quite good enough.

Frost turned the gun in his hands. Aside from giving

the pistol the brushed stainless steel look of the Metalife SS Chromium M process, Mahovsky had done a number of other things. There was a custom, ambidexterous and slightly built-up thumb safety. The slide stop was larger too—not ridiculously large and flared as some custom slide stops Frost had seen over the years, but just large enough for a firm feel when it was worked.

The magazine out of the High Power, the chamber clear, Frost snapped the trigger—no magazine safety. Aside from three new standard thirteen-round magazines to go with the gun, Frost still had numerous magazines from his old gun—there were also two twenty-round extension magazines, these Metalifed as well. This High Power was unlike his earlier guns—it sported the Browning adjustable rear sight and higher profile front sight. Mahovsky had white outlined the rear sight blade notch and placed what looked to Frost suspiciously like a Smith & Wesson red ramp insert into the front sight.

Frost took one of the twenty-round extension magazines, the magazines already loaded before he'd walked out of the house with 115-grain jacketed hollow points. He rammed the magazine up the well, his right fist wrapped around the black-checkered rubber Pachmayr grips. With his left hand—normal use of both arms almost completely restored after the woundings he'd received escaping the Soviet Union—he snapped back the High Power's slide, letting the slide ram forward.

He raised the pistol, sighting on an orange juice can Bess had liberated for him at breakfast that morning.

One-handed, unsupported, he squeezed the trigger. At what he made as thirty yards or so, the orange juice can took flight.

The one-eyed man lowered the pistol, upping the extended safety. He looked at the Metalife High Power. He verbalized it. "You did it again, Mahovsky," and he smiled. . . .

* * *

"Frost—Frost, wake up. You're dreaming—come on. It's a nightmare."

Frost shook his head, opened his eye. In the darkness of their bedroom, starlight the only light from beyond the window, he could see Bess, feel her hands holding his face.

"Do you want to talk about it?"

"Yeah—maybe—I dunno. Yeah," he nodded, kissing her lightly on the mouth and throwing his feet over the side of the bed.

He squinted as the light came on beside the bed from the small lamp there. Bess wore a floor-length white gown, the folds of the gown dropping past her ankles as she stood up, then walked across the room to get her robe.

Naked, the one-eyed man stood up.

"Here." She tossed his bathrobe across the room to him.

He caught it, then pulled it on. He glanced at the black face of the Rolex on his wrist—it was a little after three in the morning.

"You want some coffee—or will it keep you awake?"

"Yeah, coffee," he grunted.

She walked out of the room and Frost, instead of following her, walked into the bathroom. He lifted the toilet seat and practiced his marksmanship, then dropped the seat and flushed.

He stared at his face in the mirror over the bathroom sink. Since returning from Washington, despite making love with Bess frequently, he had not once slept through the night.

It was beginning to show—lines around his eye, a dark circle under it. He scratched his salt-and-pepper-stubbled face, then remembered he needed an eyepatch.

He walked back into the bedroom, cutting off the bathroom light, found his eyepatch on the nightstand beside his High Power, then pulled on the patch.

Bess was the only woman he had ever slept with without the patch.

He left the nightstand light on and walked out of the bedroom, seeing the lights on across the dark hallway that almost evenly bisected the massive old home. He walked down the hallway toward the lights, the kitchen.

He stood in the doorway, Bess turning around. She smiled, looking down toward his feet. "I got you wearing a bathrobe—now maybe I can teach you to wear slippers."

He looked down at his feet, then back into her face, then laughed. "I'm sorry. I been keepin' you awake these last weeks, haven't I?"

"No, I'm getting bags under my eyes from this clean mountain air, that's all."

"I—I—"

"I know you don't know what to do about it—sit down. The coffee's almost ready."

Almost punctuating her words he could hear the tea kettle start to whistle on the stove. She turned around to attend to it and Frost walked across the tiled floor and sat down on a stool beside the counter.

"Want it black?"

"Yeah," he nodded, finding his cigarettes and lighter on the counter top where he'd left them.

"Watch it—the coffee's hot," and she set the mug on the counter top beside him.

"Yeah," he nodded.

"Here." She took the ashtray and emptied it into the trash can, then replaced it on the counter top.

"What are you drinking?"

"Sleepy Time tea—good. You want to try some?"

"Maybe later," he nodded.

She nodded back, sitting on the stool beside him. "So, when are you gonna get help?"

"What? You mean—you mean *help* help?"

"Yes. A psychiatrist."

"You think—"

"If I did, I would have mentioned it sooner, Frost. You just can't sleep. We've talked about this before. Ever since you had that debriefing under hypnosis in Washington. Something happened. Maybe something you remembered out of your subconscious and it's trying to get to the surface and keeping you awake."

"You charge five cents for that?"

"Hell," she smiled, then took one of his cigarettes.

Frost flicked back the cowling on the Zippo, rolled the striking wheel under his thumb and moved the blue-yellow flame toward her. She nodded, exhaling through her nostrils as he closed the lighter.

"A psychiatrist could hypnotize you—just like the CIA doctors did. But only this time, you'd know what you told them."

"That might be against the law or something—national security."

"You realize how ridiculous that sounds—finding out something from the depths of your own mind is against the law? Nuts!"

"Yeah." He inhaled hard on the Camel. "You already find somebody—I mean you had to figure I'd go along with you on this, right? Or you wouldn't have mentioned it. Right?"

"I'm that obvious?"

"Only when you wanna be," he smiled.

"Yeah, I found somebody. But you don't have to go. I mean—"

He leaned across the narrow space between the two stools they occupied and kissed her lightly. "Shut up," he murmured.

Chapter Twenty-three

"What did I do while I was in seclusion at the British Embassy?" Frost echoed.

"Yes," Dr. Thurnburn said.

Frost studied the man across the desk from him. "I watched Russian soap operas," the one-eyed man began. "They imitate the successful American soaps a lot. They got one called 'Comrade Hospital.' One of my favorites though was 'Search for a Politically Acceptable Alternative to Tomorrow.' But their big hopes this season are riding on the poignant story of a group of kids who take over management of a stainless steel factory from its current capitalist ownership—they call it 'The Young and The Rustless.' "

"Is it that painful to talk about?" Dr. Thurnburn asked solicitously.

"Yeah," Frost nodded, lighting a cigarette.

"One can use hypnosis to relieve that habit as well."

"I didn't come here to change my life. I came here to find out what I should remember but can't."

"All right, Miss Stallman indicated you were a bit stubborn."

"Where would she ever get that idea?"

"Miss Stallman did an article on me several years

ago. The article brought to light some aspects of my work which have since caused considerable enhancement of my professional status. I'm doing this as a favor. I'm on vacation up here, too."

"Not 'too.' We're not on vacation in the mountains. We're hiding out from the KGB."

Thurnburn's jaw dropped. "What?"

"I guess Bess didn't tell you that part, huh?" Then Frost added, "And you can check that with her. I don't carry a gun because I'm paranoid. I carry one because I need it." Frost opened his windbreaker to show the Metalifed High Power under his left armpit in a Cobra Gunskin rig.

"Oh," and Thurnburn licked his lips, then forced a smile. "Shall we begin then. I gather I'm not the only one of us then whose time is valuable."

"Agreed," the one-eyed man nodded. "Let's get this over with."

Thurnburn nodded. "Now—there are various methods of obtaining what can be called the hypnotic state. Your job is merely to relax and let me take over. But one thing—I'd feel more comfortable and you might too if you removed your gun. Hypnotizing someone who is armed is something I've never tried and have no desire to try."

Bess was waiting in Thurnburn's living room and carried a Smith Model 60 .38 Special in her purse. Frost had bought it for her before the kidnapping.

"All right." The one-eyed man reached under his coat, dumped the High Power's magazine, and worked the slide to eject the already chambered round. He put the magazine with the chambered round reloaded into it in the pocket of his windbreaker, then set the empty gun on the desk. He wasn't worried—he always had his knife. . . .

* * *

Frost reloaded his gun, Bess sitting beside him now on a long couch, leather covered and opposite the living room windows, these looking out onto a grassy expanse disappearing into pine trees perhaps two hundred yards distant.

Thurnburn looked at his notes. "I seriously wonder if I should do something besides telling you this information—"

"Unless you got something different out of me," Frost interrupted, feeling at once both pleasantly tired and relaxed, "the guys at the CIA in Langley got the same dope."

"Comparing with what you told me afterward, there seems to be one point hypnosis brought out which your conscious mind seems to reject. Some sort of list, a list of Soviet defectors which you saw in the hospital before your escape—in the doctor's office, apparently, on his desk. I have the names here. One of them is a ballerina, but the most interesting name is Ebrahim Zuumrov."

"He's some sort of scientist," Bess said almost absently. "Let me think—he's ah—"

"Something in communications, isn't it?" Thurnburn said.

"Yes—it's blue-green laser light that—"

"Blue-green?" Frost asked. "What are you talkin' about?"

Bess looked at him, then smiled. "He was working on the same thing in the Soviet Union that some of our scientists were working on over here. The best method to use reflected blue-green laser light to communicate with submarines at their normal cruising depths. He was working on the satellite transmission of the data if I'm not mistaken."

"Captain Frost mentioned something about geosynchronous satellites being used to reflect laser light for some sort of electrodes—"

"Holy shit." Frost slumped back against the couch, finding his cigarettes, lighting one. "We've been conned," Frost said. He knew it, saw nothing he could do about it—and he was angry.

Chapter Twenty-four

Frost held Bess's hand as they walked—the feeling he had, beyond the anger, one of peace, one he hadn't known for weeks. "I never saw a list," he finally told her, standing beside the trunk of one of the pines behind their rented house.

"But—Dr. Thurnburn."

"Before we left—remember you used his bathroom? Well, I asked him if I could have been given some sort of post-hypnotic suggestion that would make me think I had seen a list when I was debriefed under hypnosis—I don't know the terminology. But he said it could have been. But it would have needed someone who was skillful. Now think about it. Why didn't I kill that doctor when I broke out of the hospital?"

"You said," she began, then looked away, "you said he'd let you see my picture."

"Sure, I owed him one. But what if it hadn't worked that way, huh? I mean, this whole thing was a set-up. Post-hypnotic suggestion again—don't kill the doctor, whatever the hell his name was."

"You mean they let you escape?" Bess stammered.

"Yeah—they let me. They put the bag on me for one reason and one reason only."

"To set you up? But why?"

Frost unfolded the Atlanta newspaper under his left arm, turned it to an inside section and showed it to her. "That's why."

" 'Prize-Winning Soviet Defector To Have Presidential Talk,' " she read. " 'Prize-winning Soviet physicist Dr. Ebrahim Zuumrov, whose defection from the Soviet Union while attending a scientific conference in Zurich, Switzerland, three months ago caused a storm of diplomatic protests from the Kremlin, will at last realize a much-talked about dream: "I have always wished to someday shake the hand of the American President." Zuumrov, who recently forced his release from a suburban Washington hospital after a mild case of food poisoning, claims his health, if anything, will be improved by the meeting. Sources close to the White House and Pentagon indicate Zuumrov brought with him what one source in the scientific community labeled "an unrealized wealth of data in the practical application of laser based communications systems." Since his defection Zuumrov has been employed by the Department of Defense, Naval Systems Engineering. This weekend's meeting will be historic in another way as well—the tightest security ever in force at Camp David since the reaching of the Camp David accords. Though White House sources remained mum, more than one highly placed Justice Department figure has observed that the KGB—the Soviet secret police and espionage agency—has a "contract" out on Zuumrov.' "

Bess put down the newspaper, looking at Frost. "That business with the hospital—the food poisoning. You think the CIA was trying to get him into a hospital in order to check for an electrode?"

"And that the Soviets have one in him? His head's a time bomb just waiting to go off and he'll kill the President?"

"Yes," she nodded.

"No," Frost told her. "No—it was all a scam. Otherwise, why the fake list? And if those electrodes work so well, then why the hell didn't Arika Gorki do more than be a pain in the ass. Why didn't she kill me, turn me in—something?"

"I don't follow you," Bess murmured, looking blankly at him.

"They set me up—all the way. That electrode Burns' people at CIA pulled out of Arika's brain. At least according to what Burns said, nobody could figure just how it worked."

"Wait a minute—come on." Bess started running toward the house. Frost started after her, across the grass and onto the redwood deck, then through the old french doors into the dining room, then after her into the kitchen. When he reached the kitchen, she had the telephone to her left ear, holding an earring in her right hand. "If my memory is right—then you're right," Bess said. "Give me a cigarette."

Frost nodded, finding his Camels in his shirt pocket, then lighting two of them.

He handed her one and she nodded, then through a cloud of smoke said into the receiver, "Give me Harry Elms at the Foreign Desk. Thanks."

"You want some coffee?" Frost asked her.

She just shook her head, then whispered loudly, "Drink?"

"Sounds good to me." The one-eyed man nodded, then started to find the liquor under the counter.

He found a bottle of vodka—but suddenly had no taste for it. He took out the Seagrams Seven and found two glasses, then walked to the refrigerator—Bess was talking to someone on the phone. "Yeah, Harry, that's right. Bess Stallman. How have you been? . . . Listen—got a favor to ask . . . Yeah, a story I'm working on. This Zuumrov guy—the scientist? . . . Yeah . . . Somewhere at the back of my mind I remember Zuumrov was in a motorcycle accident about six or seven years ago . . . It was ten years ago? I'm getting old . . . That's it—that's it, Harry. Thank you . . . You, too!" and she blew a kiss into the receiver, then hung up.

"Here," and Frost handed her a glass of Seagrams on the rocks.

"You were right—it is some kind of set-up." Bess smiled as she sipped at the whiskey.

"What'd you find out about Zuumrov?"

"That motorcycle accident? That's what I thought I remembered out back. He has a steel plate in his head. If he had an electrode implant, nobody'd be able to tell without an operation. X-rays wouldn't penetrate the steel plate."

"And Zuumrov would naturally insist he never had an electrode implanted because if he had, he wouldn't know about it anyway."

"But why are they still letting him see the President this weekend?"

The one-eyed man downed his drink. "How about this headline," he rasped: "KGB Assassinates Soviet Scientist En Route To Presidential Meeting."

"You mean—"

"The KGB couldn't get to him—otherwise he would have been dead a long time ago. But the CIA will get to him—or some agency. And set it up to look like the KGB did it."

Bess sipped again at her drink. "So our government will carry out an assassination for the KGB."

He felt bitter, tired—angrier than before. "And I did everything but pull the trigger," Frost snarled.

Chapter Twenty-five

Frost walked quickly, despite the pain in his leg. O'Hara, walking beside him, snapped, "If you hadn't been in such a big hurry, I coulda found us a closer spot to park."

"I can't wait," Frost answered, out of breath a little. Ahead of them was a massive apartment structure, part of a still more massive complex. Frost stopped beside the base of the steps. "Give me that little gun you carry in the ankle holster."

"Where's your gun?"

"My fault D.C.'s got dumb gun laws? I couldn't bring it."

O'Hara glanced behind him, then stooped over quickly, popping the Model 60 Smith & Wesson Chief's stainless from the holster on the inside of his left ankle. "Here." He palmed the gun to Frost, the one-eyed man stuffing it under the sportcoat he wore, and into the waistband of his trousers. "Take this, too," O'Hara handed him a cylinder-shaped Safariland Speed Loader.

"What you got in here?"

"Some of the old Smith Nyclads—works good."

Frost only nodded, then started up the steps. Arika Gorki had taken an apartment in the building nearly two weeks earlier, under an assumed name. Taking up a lot of favors, after Frost had called him, O'Hara had found out the name and address.

At the entrance near the mailboxes and the call buttons, Frost stopped. "You wanna wait outside—I mean, I know you can get in more trouble doin' this than I can."

"No, I'll come in."

Frost nodded, then found the call button for "Andrea Garrett," then rang. He heard no answering buzz opening the door into the lobby, no static over the intercom. He rang again and waited.

The one-eyed man looked over his shoulder, then fished his wallet out of his hip pocket. He took a credit card and worked it on the locking mechanism of the glass door. "This won't work on her door most likely," Frost said absently, talking as he pried the credit card between the lock and the jamb.

"What are we lookin' for anyway?" O'Hara asked. "What—a Russian spy union card or somethin'?"

Frost looked at O'Hara, then laughed. "Maybe—I'll know when I find it, if I find it." Frost tugged at the glass door—it opened.

"Come on." He started through, the pain in his leg starting again as he walked. Her apartment was on the eighteenth floor and Frost didn't even remotely consider his dislike for elevators.

He punched the elevator button.

"Good thing this joint doesn't have keys for the elevators," O'Hara remarked.

Frost said nothing, stepping in as the elevator doors opened, then punching the button for the eighteenth floor. "You got gloves?" Frost asked.

"Why—what? Fingerprints?"

"Yeah."

"I'm a cop. What've I gotta worry about?" O'Hara

grinned sheepishly.

"Here," and Frost reached into a side jacket pocket and produced a pair of thin black leather gloves. "Pretend you're left-handed." Frost gave O'Hara the left glove. He felt the elevator stop then, the doors opening, then he stepped out into the corridor.

The corridor was like a long, narrow, low-ceilinged concrete box, painted white.

"Eyuch!" Frost remarked, then scanned the door numbers, finding the pattern, turning right and walking along the doors, looking for Arika's apartment.

He stopped in front of the door—"18F"—and began fishing into his pockets.

"Whatchya lookin' for?"

"The lock pick set."

"I gave it to you," O'Hara admonished.

"I know—I know," Frost came back, annoyed. "You know how to use one of these things?" he said finally.

"No, when you asked me to bring one, I figured you knew how."

"Oh—wonderful," Frost rasped. He opened the little black leather pouch, having no idea which of the dozen picks would be the right one for the lock. He took one, bent to the door and started to work, saying, "Give me back the other glove—I'll need it here." Pulling it on with this teeth, his right hand working the pick, Frost could taste the leather dye as he tried turning the knob. "Oh great," Frost snapped, holding up the pick. "I broke the damn pick!"

"Try another one—looks like you got a lot to choose from."

Frost didn't say anything. He had nothing else he could do but try another one. He selected one at random, tried inserting it in the lock and found it wouldn't go. "Can't be that one," he said aloud to himself, then took another pick. He placed it in the locking mechanism and twisted, the pick bending, but as he turned the knob, the door gave.

"All right," O'Hara laughed. "See—I knew you could do it. Little Yankee ingenuity and—"

"Aw, shut up," Frost snapped. He wasn't in the mood. He started through the doorway, not knowing what he'd find. "Oh, boy," Frost moaned, turning around and looking back into the hallway.

"What's the matter?" It was O'Hara, the lanky FBI man passing him. "Aw, shit," O'Hara whispered.

The one-eyed man turned to look back into the apartment.

Frost couldn't remember the guy's first name. But the last name was Burns. He was the CIA man Frost had been debriefed by, the man Frost had called to warn about Arika Gorki and the assassination of Zuumrov. "Looks like he was too good an agent," O'Hara observed, "but not too good with a gun."

On the floor in the middle of the apartment living room, Burns had been dead for at least several hours. Blue lines were visible where the veins in his face and hands had pumped blood before death, now the blood had stopped. The left eye was still there, but the right one was gone and on the floor under the back of the head was a large dark stain that Frost guessed was blood mixed with brain matter.

There was a worn blue Detective Special in Burns' right hand, and a dead cigar in his left. "I think he was tiring of the way those cigars tasted anyway," Frost remarked, instantly feeling callous for saying it.

Chapter Twenty-six

Frost had used the gloves to wipe off the downstairs door handle, even the call button on the elevator on the first floor, the doorbell by the mailbox, and the outer hallway door handle. Then with O'Hara looking over his shoulder awkwardly and Frost murmuring to him, "Relax," they started walking.

"Relax? How the hell can I relax? That wasn't just an ordinary stiff. That was Burns—big guy in CIA. And you tell me to relax?"

Frost handed O'Hara back the stainless-steel Chiefs Special and the speedloader.

O'Hara made the revolver disappear under his jacket as they passed a woman walking down the street. "You trying to get the cops onto us?"

"You are the cops," Frost reminded him.

"Then why the hell wouldn't you let me call anybody?"

"No time—gotta figure her next move—and quick. Before she kills Zuumrov. Or I could be all wrong. Maybe Zuumrov has an electrode in his head and plans to kill the President or something."

O'Hara stepped off the curb, walking behind the F.O.U.O. American Motors sedan and getting in. As he leaned across the front seat to pop the lock, Frost climbed in.

"Let's grab some coffee where we can talk," Frost told him.

"There's a place a couple of blocks from here I know."

O'Hara cut the wheel sharp left, then Frost snapped forward as he felt O'Hara hit the brakes. The one-eyed man glanced over his left shoulder as he heard the horn. "You almost hit that van, Mike. Relax, will ya?"

O'Hara stomped the gas pedal, cutting in ahead of the van. "I'm relaxed already—can't ya see I'm relaxed."

The one-eyed man closed his eye. Driving with O'Hara, it was better that way. . . .

Frost sipped at the steaming coffee on the counter in the truck stop—it was one of O'Hara's favorite places and he tried talking the one-eyed man into trying the chili. Frost had had dysentery once. He passed after catching a glimpse of the kitchen through the swinging doors. But he figured the coffee would be hot enough to disinfect the cup. O'Hara had been on the phone for more than ten minutes, already two people having come up to the single pay phone, waited looking progressively more angry and impatient, then left.

Frost turned on the stool, watching now as a third man—huge, with a trucker's wallet chained to his belt and stuffed in the right jeans pocket, his arm muscles flexed beneath the rolled up work shirt sleeves—tapped O'Hara's shoulder. O'Hara gave him a grin then returned to the telephone. The man tapped again, then loudly snarled, "You been on the damn phone here for more than ten minutes, pal—get off. Ya read the sign—public phone?"

O'Hara snapped, "Get lost, huh—government business," and started to turn away.

"Government, my ass—I'm a taxpayer. Go use your own phone, mac!"

He grabbed at O'Hara's right shoulder, turning him around. O'Hara, his face registering disgust, reached under his coat and pulled his I.D. case, flashing it to the trucker. "FBI—got business here. Relax," and O'Hara started to put away his I.D., the trucker—Frost guessed he was having a bad day or something—didn't say anything. He grabbed O'Hara's right shoulder, spinning him around.

The trucker's mouth opened—wide. Less than two inches from his chest was the muzzle of O'Hara's Metalifed Model 29 .44 Magnum. "I said I got business, but I'll be off the phone in a couple of minutes. Okay?"

The trucker nodded once, turned around and walked away, O'Hara making the gun disappear.

Frost returned to his coffee, cooler now. He lit a cigarette. If Burns had had second thoughts when Frost had warned him of a KGB set-up, then—the one-eyed man tried putting it together. Burns had come to see Arika, perhaps coming exactly the same way Frost and O'Hara had come—unannounced. Arika had surprised him, then shot him. Burns had found, heard or seen something incriminating, already had his gun out.

Frost shook his head.

He felt someone tap him on the shoulder and spun on the stool, thinking maybe it was the trucker.

But it was O'Hara. "I found out what we needed to know."

"What?"

"Come on out to the car—can't tell you here." Frost only nodded, putting a buck on the counter for his coffee and O'Hara's—untouched—and standing up to follow O'Hara. Frost saw it, but O'Hara didn't, the trucker's foot snapping out in O'Hara's path, O'Hara walking into it. O'Hara started to fall, catching himself from sprawling to the floor by grabbing the back of a metal-framed chair at one of the center tables.

"Gee—sorry, pal," the trucker said, then laughed to his friends in the booth.

O'Hara stood fully erect.

Frost stepped between O'Hara and the trucker's table. There was a large mug of coffee on the table in front of the trucker and Frost picked it up, then tossed it down on the man's shirt front. The trucker jumped to his feet, yelling with the pain from the hot coffee against his skin, then reaching out his hands toward Frost's throat. The one-eyed man sidestepped left, feigning a straight right, the trucker dodging right to avoid it. Frost's left fist swung up, the knuckles catching at the tip of the man's jaw, sending him sprawling back across the table. "Gee—sorry, pal," Frost said. He pushed O'Hara ahead of him and started for the door.

"You're in a bad mood," O'Hara laughed as they got through the doorway onto the sidewalk. "I coulda put that guy away."

"You're a Fed—you'd get in trouble. Me—not as much. Don't worry about it. Anyway, I figured I needed some limbering up." Frost started toward the car, parked half a block down at the curb, his left leg hurting not much but enough that he couldn't forget about it. "What'd you find out?"

"Nobody advertises this sorta thing, and we were on an open line, but I got hold of a friend in clandestine work with the Company. Seems like Burns had hired three guys—might be syndicate types, maybe independent contractors, but triggermen. Then yesterday Burns was tryin' to get hold of the three guys, but couldn't."

"He was settin' 'em up?" Frost remarked, stopping beside the car.

"Couldn't use Company people just in case they got

caught—that's all I think it was. But the clincher is Arika what's-her-name—"

"Gorki," Frost interjected.

"Yeah, Gorki. Well, she and Burns were lovers."

"What?" Frost shook his head. "They were lovers?"

"Before the Gorki dame left for Moscow three years ago, and since she got back. They both had the same security clearances, so nobody said anything. She isn't Russian-born anyway, and she isn't a contract employee—she's a case officer." O'Hara didn't make to open the car. "And I did some other checkin'. Seems like at least one time Arika Gorki had to kill somebody in the line of duty—you know, him-or-me type thing. She shot the guy in the right eye—supposed to be one of the best people with a pistol in the whole agency. Used to compete before she went overseas."

"Oh, shit," Frost murmured, shaking his head. "This was more of a set-up than I figured."

"Burns was probably a Commie, figured you were onto him, meaning you'd put me onto him."

"No," Frost mused. "No—I'll buy him maybe being a Communist, or maybe just entrapped by one—Arika, you know? Let's say—" and Frost nodded, more to himself than to O'Hara. "Let's run this one. Say Burns was a good loyal guy, then suddenly found himself compromised with Arika when it turned out she was a Red. Maybe a family involved, or maybe just figured he'd lose his top security clearance. So, he winds up working with her, mainly just covering up for her, and when she's shipped out—maybe he even arranged it—she'd be less of a threat to him. But she comes back on this electrode deal. She has one implanted in her brain—but it's a phoney, a good phoney."

"I don't follow you," O'Hara said, shaking his head. "Why all the trouble for a phoney electrode in the first place?"

"Same reason they hijacked me," Frost answered, lighting a Camel in the blue-yellow flame of his battered Zippo. "All part of the groundwork to get our guys to assassinate Zuumrov. Let's say the Russians really were working on this electrode deal. But when Zuumrov defected, their chance of using the electrode thing was shot to hell because he was the only guy who could have gotten that blue-green laser light stuff to signal the electrodes and activate the people who were wearin' 'em in their heads. So—a couple hundred million rubles out the window. 'But wait a minute,' some crafty little KGB guy says, 'we can use the electrode dodge to put Zuumrov away.' "

"What?"

"Think about it. Our intelligence would probably confirm the electrode thing because that was an established project. They put the bag on me, let me escape. They even let me shoot my way out killing a lot of their people, just to make it look authentic. I come stateside, tell my story, then even give 'em a list of the defectors with the electrode implants. Why the hell would the list have been written in English in the first place? They coulda had my name up in a neon sign and I wouldn't a been able to read it in Cyrillic alphabet! So I finger Zuumrov, to a man who already knows I'm gonna do it. He pushed for termination after they check Zuumrov in the hospital, find out about the plate in his head and realize they can't get at the electrode without Zuumrov screamin' his head off. Sure he says he doesn't have one. If he did, he wouldn't know it. And they probably knew he was workin' on the electrode project, so they wouldn't have asked him anyway—they'd expect a lie. Got this guy working in some super-secret stuff on communications with nuclear submarines. Maybe he's been feedin' it all to the Russians and the defection was a cover for a KGB tie-up. And, maybe the electrode thing works already and Zuumrov's a walkin' bomb that can be triggered to kill the President. What would you do?"

"Ice him—make it look like the KGB did it."

"Sure—so you hire some stateside killers and give 'em the target. Probably that was Burns' idea. But you send a CIA operative along—who's better than an American-born Russian woman who has three years or so in the Soviet Union behind her—just peg her as a double. Then Burns is rid of Arika and he's off the hook and can go back to bein' a good Fed again."

"But then you called. He figured the operation had to be stopped, so he went to smoke Arika."

"And she killed him," Frost nodded.

"So Arika and those hired torpedoes are still out there lookin' for Zuumrov."

"I don't think they're lookin' very hard. You're gonna have to find out his route this afternoon."

O'Hara looked back toward the diner. "Let's find a different phone this time though, huh?"

Chapter Twenty-seven

Phone calls from a gas station three blocks away had made Frost realize he was either a genius or thoroughly perverted to have psyched the KGB plot. Zuumrov had never been asked about the electrode implant—if he had, Zuumrov could have explained that it was impossible with the current state of Soviet technology, even in a laboratory, Frost theorized. Burns had indeed hired three men—the two De Soto brothers from Las Vegas and Vincent Carrillo. Carillo had several times been investigated by the Justice Department in association with gangland killings, and the De Soto brothers were graduates of several prison systems after plea-bargaining their way out of involvement in syndicate-related muscle operations—murder, arson, aggravated battery. No one at CIA—according to what O'Hara discerned—had quite known the source of Burns' contacts with the men. And Arika had been scheduled to accompany the hit team. The last piece of information had been the hardest to get because O'Hara's boss at FBI had gotten a member of the Senate Select Committee on Intelligence to get it out of a CIA Deputy Director. Admitting to a planned assassination, let alone on American soil, was nothing anyone had been eager to do.

Frost stood beside O'Hara's car, digesting the last piece of information. Arika knew the route; Zuumrov had already started on it and it was too late to pull the plug on the Secret Service people escorting Zuumrov. To attract less attention, they were not taking the advertised route and would keep their radios off until and unless a situation developed where they needed to contact headquarters. Otherwise, unless the Secret Service initiated contact, there would be no contact possible.

"The Bureau's got helicopters going out across the route now to try and flag 'em. It'll probably work."

"And what if it doesn't?" Frost asked.

"They'll never get into Camp David, so the President's okay anyway."

"What about Zuumrov—and the Secret Service men guarding him?"

"My guys are gonna do the best they can."

"And even if they flag down the Secret Service and rescue Zuumrov, then Arika still gets away clean. Get back on the phone to your boss."

"What?" O'Hara looked totally perplexed.

"There's another way—I think." The one-eyed man started back across the service station's oil-stained concrete apron, toward the telephone. It wasn't just another way, he thought—it was the only way....

The helicopter landing in the vacant lot beside the service station had caused a stir, raised eyebrows, questions. Frost and O'Hara had ignored them all, running to board the little bubble-domed Bell and getting airborne as quickly as possible.

Over the noise of the rotors overhead, Frost heard and felt the tapping against his ear. He turned and looked at O'Hara, sitting behind him, Frost himself sitting opposite the pilot. O'Hara was shouting something and Frost raised the protective earphone he wore. "You're crazy—more I think about it!"

"Tell me somethin' new," Frost shouted back, then laughed. He bent forward, scanning the road ahead of them, watching the helicopter's shadow, Frost's eye searching for ... he saw it, tapping the pilot on the shoulder and pointing below them. The Navy pilot nodded once and gestured downward, the helicopter almost immediately beginning to descend. The target was an F.O.U.O. car parked at the crossroads of a dirt farm road and a two-lane highway below them. Frost released his seat belt before he felt the touchdown in the pit of his stomach.

He shot the Navy pilot a wave, then started out of the chopper, glancing once behind him, seeing O'Hara running after him. A man stood beside the F.O.U.O. car, a perplexed look on his face.

"O'Hara!" the lanky FBI man shouted, breathless, flashing his I.D. to the man beside the car.

"Dirkens—I'm with the Department of Agriculture. What the hell is going on here?"

"You just had the closest car, pal—take a helicopter ride."

The man named Dirkens just shook his head in a "What-the-hell" attitude and started to jog toward the Navy helicopter.

Frost slipped down into the driver's seat, O'Hara running in front of the car, Frost starting the engine. O'Hara was still climbing in as Frost threw the car into gear, then cut the wheel into a hard right as he fed the car the gas, turning it up the dirt road. "You sure this thing connects with the highway Zuumrov's on?"

"Unless the Secret Service didn't know what it was talkin' about when they told my boss," O'Hara answered. "You mind telling me how two of us are gonna take four of them with only two guns between us, one of 'em a peashooter?"

"Our hearts are pure," Frost smiled. Cranking the wheel into a tight right then back left, he avoided a chuckhole. He glanced down at the speedometer—over seventy—then into the rearview mirror, at the dust cloud behind them.

"I don't see how the hell you talked anybody into lettin' us try this stunt," O'Hara said, shaking his head as Frost looked across toward him.

"Easy," Frost told him. "Just gave 'em a logical choice. Send a chopper to flag down Zuumrov and you lose Arika, the De Sota brothers and Carrillo—leave 'em out there to try some other plan maybe, maybe track down Zuumrov some other time."

"Yeah, but maybe they got a bomb or somethin'. How they plannin' to stop a car, anyway?"

"Try workin' as a merc sometime, Mike, I know there are lots of ways. Betchya Arika knows 'em all."

"I just hope we get there in time to spot 'em and switch cars—otherwise we got a dead Zuumrov."

Frost didn't say anything—he was too busy goosing the speedometer past eighty and dodging potholes. . . .

Frost skidded the car across the highway, blocking it, the black Cadillac Fleetwood skidding too, then starting a high speed reverse as O'Hara jumped from the car Frost drove, running toward it. O'Hara's badge was in his outstretched right fist. There was a solid chance the driver of Zuumrov's car wouldn't take the initiative to stop, a better chance somebody from the front passenger seat would open fire.

The Cadillac skidded into a flick turn, out of the reverse, starting away, O'Hara standing in the middle of the road, shouting, "FBI—wait up!"

The Cadillac miraculously stopped. No one exited the car. Frost climbed out of the F.O.U.O. car and raised his hands high. "Mike—put your hands up—show 'em we're not goin' for anything!"

O'Hara turned around for a second, then raised both hands, still holding his badge high.

"FBI—I got a message for you from Mr. Zeiter, your boss. My name's O'Hara. Get on the damn radio," O'Hara shouted. From the distance, Frost couldn't tell if the Cadillac had an open window or not, if anyone could hear O'Hara.

"Start walkin' toward the car. Keep showin' 'em the badge," Frost recommended, starting himself to walk toward it.

The distance to the Cadillac was perhaps two hundred yards as Frost—limping—moved toward it. The back door suddenly opened and the passenger side front door as well, two men in three-piece suits exiting, what looked at the distance like Uzi subguns in their hands.

Frost called out. "My name is Frost—his is O'Hara. FBI sent us. So did your boss, Floyd Zeiter. Call him on the radio. We're not movin' on ya!"

The man from the front seat turned to the man standing beside the rear door. The second man nodded and the man from the front seat climbed back inside.

"Twitch and you're both all over the road," the man from the back seat called. Frost almost nodded to answer him. But he waited instead.

Chapter Twenty-eight

There was always the possibility, Frost realized, that Arika knew what frequency the Secret Service would use if it did make contact. And she knew that Zuumrov and the Secret Service guards were using the Department of Agriculture F.O.U.O. car now to get Zuumrov back down the dusty farmroad and to the next highway grid and to a Maryland State Police rendezvous and a helicopter that would fly Zuumrov to Camp David. But even so, Frost felt somehow Arika would hang on, keep the De Soto brothers and Vincent Carrillo on tap with their assault rifles and whatever else they had ready to stop the car—maybe just to get even.

"We shoulda taken both squirt guns," O'Hara observed, the Cadillac moving under his hands at what Frost judged an even fifty or fifty-five.

Frost reinserted the Uzi's magazine, then opened the bolt and applied the safety. "Couldn't leave those guys with just their handguns," Frost commented. "Anyway—you got two handguns, and I've got this now."

"Yeah, and what if they've got a bazooka and just blow the car up?"

"I don't think so," Frost nodded. "Arika's gotta be certain she gets Zuumrov. And if she blows up the car, she won't be sure, never would be. Gotta be more traditional. She'll want to stop us somehow, then kill everybody in the car. Just 'cause that happens to be us, isn't anything we should hold against her."

"You talk about me and *my* logic," O'Hara cracked.

"Up ahead!" Frost shouted, a dark green sedan coming toward them, cutting across the highway, a massive, add-on bumper all but obscuring the hood, a wire cage surrounding the bumper.

"Gonna ram us!" O'Hara shouted. "Look out!" Frost braced himself with the passenger grab handle as O'Hara worked the emergency brake, cutting the wheel hard left. The Cadillac skidded under them. The car lurched as the emergency brake was released, then Frost could hear the steadily increasing roar as the Cadillac's engine cranked RPMs, O'Hara's foot—as Frost glanced toward him—pressed down to the floor.

The one-eyed man craned his neck to look behind them. "You got this thing dead out?" Frost shouted.

"Pretty much," O'Hara answered.

"Then that guy's got a big worked over V-8 in there. He's gaining on us."

"Shit," O'Hara snapped, and Frost felt the Cadillac start to shudder; apparently O'Hara was pushing the car to its limits.

Frost heard it before he saw it in the sideview, then turned around again—gunfire from the green car with the massive bumper. "Relax—armor plate," O'Hara called out. The rear window of the Cadillac was spider-webbing. "Tell that to them," Frost snapped.

"Must be usin' armor-piercing stuff."

"No kiddin'!" Frost tucked down, a burst of automatic weapons fire shattering the rear window completely now, glass spraying across the back seat into the front seat.

"Aww—dammit!" It was O'Hara, the car weaving

now, the FBI man's left hand clutching at the back of his neck, blood oozing between his fingers.

"Get down!" Frost raised the Uzi over the seat back, steadying it there as best he could, opening up, a nice, controlled three-shot burst going toward the green sedan less than twenty-five yards behind them.

"I hit it. I know I hit it. Can't get past that damn bumper," Frost shouted.

"My neck, Frost. I'm bleeding heavy. Head—hurtin' bad. Maybe gonna pass out," O'Hara shouted. "In front of us!"

The one-eyed man wheeled forward, then punched the button for the passenger side window to lower. A second car, identical to the first was coming straight toward them.

"Hang on, Mike—they got us boxed in!"

"I'm hittin' the radio." O'Hara—Frost glanced toward him for an instant—snatched up the microphone. The one-eyed man shoved the Uzi out the passenger side front window, aiming it toward the green bumper car coming toward them, trying to get a clear sight over the massive bumper and cage. He fired anyway, hearing O'Hara shouting into the microphone, "This is O'Hara in the Cadillac—under attack thirty-five miles outside Camp David on—" There was a long burst of automatic weapons fire and O'Hara almost screamed the word, "Dammit!"

Frost glanced left. The radio set under the dashboard was shot out, the seat back between them almost shredded. "What the hell they usin', Frost? You know all this exotic weapons shit."

The one-eyed man leveled a burst at the advancing green car in front of him. "Must be some specially made-up armor piercing .22s—only thing could penetrate armor like this. I've seen .22 subguns before—maybe they got one."

"Wonderful. This'll look great on my damn record—O'Hara shot down by a dinky .22!"

"That guy's cutting us off," Frost warned, trying to steady the Uzi as O'Hara hit the emergency brake. The car skidded into a flick turn, the green car weaving into the other lane. There was a clear shot—for an instant only—and Frost took it, firing out what he guessed was half a magazine into the driver's side front and rear windows. The green car disappeared from sight as Frost was whiplashed back against the seat, the Cadillac completing the turn. He heard the long popping sound of the emergency brake being let off, then the engine roaring again.

Frost twisted in the seat, looking behind them now toward the second green car. It was gone, along the near shoulder of the road, overended. "All right!" Frost hammered his left fist against the dashboard. "Got the sucker!"

"Get this one—huh?"

Frost looked forward, the original green car coming for them dead on. "I flick-turn outa this and he'll broadside us. And I'm goin' too fast for a reverse—watch it!"

O'Hara cut the wheel hard left, Frost ducking down across the seat, hearing the tearing sound of metal against metal, the massive bumper of the green car impacting against them. O'Hara shouted something Frost couldn't understand, then there was the roaring of the engine again, Frost feeling the Cadillac lurch ahead.

The one-eyed man was up, twisting around in the seat, poking the Uzi out the passenger side window. The green car was making a wide U-turn, starting after them again, someone leaning out of the front passenger window, firing something that looked like a gun from a science-fiction movie. Frost watched almost spellbound as the bullet holes ripped their way toward him along the body of the Cadillac.

Frost fired the Uzi, emptying the magazine, dropping it out the window then tucking back inside as the gunfire from the green car tore through the front passenger door. Bullet holes opened in the glove compartment door and the dashboard; the sideview mirror on the passenger side was sheared away.

"Gotta stop that subgunner!" Frost shouted, then looked toward O'Hara. The back of O'Hara's suit was stained with blood, O'Hara slumped across the steering wheel barely holding on. The one-eyed man reached across with his left hand, pushing O'Hara's head back. O'Hara— nearly unconscious it seemed to Frost—slumped back against the seat. The Cadillac started slicing across the road, toward the near shoulder as Frost snatched at the steering wheel, his left fist on it, cutting the wheel hard left to pull the Cadillac back into the highway.

The one-eyed man edged left, trying to get his left foot to where he could control the gas pedal and the brakes, kicking O'Hara's right foot away from the gas. The Cadillac was already slowing.

Frost started pumping the brake, the green car slowing behind them.

There was only one chance—and he had to take it. Throwing his body across O'Hara to protect his friend as much as possible, Frost punched his left foot down on the emergency brake, cutting the wheel all the way hard left. He felt the car skidding, then reached up, cutting the wheel back right.

He felt the impact, the green car with its massive bumper hammering into the Cadillac's rear end; he felt the shuddering of the Cadillac's body and frame, heard the ripping of metal, the shattering of glass. Then the rolling came. Frost hugged O'Hara against him as the Cadillac spun and toppled. Then the bone shattering-feeling, the scraping sounds—and then the gasoline fumes as the motion of the car stopped.

Frost looked up, feeling glass falling from him as he moved. The front windshield was gone. Frost reached across, finding the door handle—there was something wrong. He suddenly realized the Cadillac was upside down. Frost wrenched at the handle, the door popping open. Frost pushed himself across the fabric roof, dragging O'Hara behind him, across the door frame and onto the pavement.

He could smell smoke now as well as fumes. The one-eyed man, not yet knowing if anything on his own body was broken or bleeding, hauled O'Hara up onto his right shoulder, then started toward the ditch along the side of the road.

Instinct told him to hit the dirt. He hurtled O'Hara down, then covered the FBI man with his own body. The roar behind him deafened him for an instant, a blast of hot air that smelled of gasoline washing over him, almost robbing him of breath.

Shaking his head to clear it, Frost snatched at the shoulder holster under O'Hara's bloodied jacket, finding the Pachmayr-gripped butt of the customized Model 29.

He ripped the gun clear of the leather, turning around on his knees. From the other side of the massive fireball, Frost saw one man, and a second one behind him, the two men almost as alike-looking as bookends. The De Soto brothers, he guessed.

Above the crackling of the flames, Frost could hear the tromboning of a pump shotgun—the man furthest forward had one. The one behind had the space-age sub-machine gun.

Frost leveled O'Hara's .44 Magnum and fired, the massive N-Frame rocking in his hands. The shotgun in the nearer of the De Soto brothers' hands discharged into the tarmac of the road surface.

The .22 subgun was firing, a long burst; the road surface and ground inches ahead of Frost was chewed up under it. Frost didn't move—he could have rolled, but O'Hara would have taken the burst. Frost felt something tearing at his coat but he brought the six-inch Metalifed Model 29 down out of the recoil, holding it tighter this time, double-actioning the smooth trigger. The gun roared again in his hands, the .22 subgun suddenly firing skyward the second De Soto's body twisted, then tumbled back.

The one-eyed man—now that the Cadillac was still burning less than twenty-five yards from him, and the two almost-dead men were twitching on the ground—stood up. He held the Model 29 limply along his right thigh, his wrist hurting from the unaccustomed recoil.

There was no more movement, no one else out there.

Quickly, Frost bent to O'Hara—there was still a pulse and at least some of O'Hara's radio message had gotten through, he was sure. Help would be there. He could feel it.

Frost started walking toward the other green car. As he walked, he thumb-cocked the Model 29, still leaving it hanging at his side.

He stopped, ten yards from the car. He raised the muzzle of the Smith toward the face beside the steering wheel, then lowered the revolver's hammer. There was no need to waste a bullet. Vincent Carrillo had a broken neck. But where was Arika Gorki?

Chapter Twenty-nine

There had been a private meeting with a United States Senator from the Intelligence Committee, and an even more private meeting with Zuumrov. Dr. Ebrahim Zuumrov had perhaps fared the worst of any of them. O'Hara had been wounded by glass fragments, not bullets, and was all but recovered. Frost had not been wounded by the burst from the submachine gun, but the left side of his coattail was shredded. The De Soto brothers and Carrillo had finally performed their finest service for humanity—by being dead.

But Zuumrov—the KGB would be after him forever. And by his own choice, rather than submerge his identity, he would live under constant guard. That was the only way he could perform his work. And his work with the blue-green laser light communications system would not be completed for at least a decade, perhaps longer.

Frost sat in his reclining chair, the sounds of Bess fixing dinner once again in the background. O'Hara—back on marginal duty—had promised to contact him if Arika were spotted and somehow get him in on the finish if there were one. Frost doubted O'Hara'd be able to keep the promise.

Arika had, indeed, murdered Burns, and Burns had been her unwilling accomplice for five years—sexual blackmail. A wife, three school-age children, a security clearance, and little money in the bank—it had added up to deception, then finally death, for the man after five years of treason. To his credit, Burns had helped his Soviet masters as little as possible.

Frost smoked a cigarette, pitying Burns suddenly—a patriot, a loyal American to begin with, forced into treason. The one-eyed man inhaled hard, wondering how some people lived with their own guts.

"Frost, come and eat."

The one-eyed man stood up, looking back across the room at Bess. She had a massive platter in her pot-holdered hands. She was setting it on the dinette table, the table covered with a lace cloth and lit candles.

"This is a rerun of that dinner we tried to have—the welcome home dinner," she told him. "And I don't care if a dozen guys break down the door this time—shoot 'em fast so we can eat."

Frost stood beside her, his arm around her. Thinly sliced steaks, over a steaming bed of wild rice, surrounded in a circle by asparagus spears filled the platter. "I've got an apple pie in the oven—I even made it myself," she smiled, looking up at him.

"I love you," he told her quietly, then kissed her forehead.

"Eat—before it gets cold."

"Only if I get two desserts," he told her.

"Two pieces of pie?" she asked as he held her chair for her.

"Maybe—but after that dessert . . ." He leaned over, whispering into her ear.

The lights were off in the bedroom. Frost had hit the

light switch as soon as he'd entered the room.

"I'm not undressed," she complained.

"I'll fix that," he murmured, taking her into his arms. He felt her hands touching his face; he heard and felt her breath. "See, I'm fixing it already."

"Hmm," she purred. Frost fumbled with the hook and eye closure at the back of her dress, then found the tab of the zipper. "How's the journalism business? That was some dinner with you working all day."

"If you married me and made this all legal I could make dinners like that every night," she whispered.

"One of these days," he said, working the zipper down the length of her back. He started to search for the closure of her bra, but couldn't find it.

"Hmm—you didn't watch me get dressed this morning, did you," she whispered in his ear. "I'm wearing one that closes in the front."

"Very sneaky," he told her, reaching up to the shoulders of her dress, pulling them forward and down along her arms, the sleeves catching at her wrists.

"I've got buttons there, you know. You'll have to undo them."

"Hmm—maybe," he said. He drifted his fingers down across her shoulders and across the upper portions of her breasts. At her cleavage, he found what he guessed had to be the bra's fastener, fumbled it in his fingers and released it.

"Now what are you going to do? You can't get me out of the bra until you get my wrists out of the dress," she told him.

"Just come and stretch out across the bed and don't worry about it," and he walked her across the darkened room, moonlight flooding it in gray slats across the carpet. He sat her down on the edge of the bed, then pushed her back, feeling her wriggle her legs onto the bed, feeling her edge closer beside him. He took her face in his hands, touching his lips to her eyelids, then to the tip of her nose, then to her lips, lingering there, her mouth pressing against his, opening, their tongues meeting.

She pushed away, raising her hands between them. "The buttons?"

"The buttons," he repeated, finding the cuff buttons. They seemed to be covered with the fabric of the dress and there were three on each wrist. He opened them, then pulled the dress down from her arms.

"It goes off over my head," she whispered.

Frost pulled it up, feeling her shake it loose, then feeling her hands at his crotch.

He helped her the rest of the way free of the bra as he felt her unzipping his pants, felt her hands going inside, holding him.

He moved around so she could pull them off, then felt her as she laid across him, her hands undoing the buttons of his shirt.

"I've got cuff buttons too," he told her.

"I know," she came back. "I'll get them."

She did.

He rolled her onto her back, pushing down the half slip and panties she wore, sliding them along her thighs, down her calves and over her ankles, her legs still encased in the stockings like she habitually wore, the kind that stayed on her thighs as if magically defying gravity.

He watched the gray outline of her as she sat up suddenly, drawing up her right leg, the knee almost touching her chin. Her hands moved down along her thighs and along her calf, pushing down the stocking. Then she did the same with her left leg, Frost stripping his shirt the rest of the way.

With both of them naked, he took her into his arms, his mouth coming down on hers, his left hand touching her right breast, his fingertips brushing against the nipple.

He felt her hands on him, moving against him as he slipped on top of her, between her legs, her fingers guiding him into her.

His arms folded around her, her abdomen feeling tight against his, her body seeming to rise under his. For a long time, until they sank together, they remained locked in each other's arms . . .

The phone was ringing; the one-eyed man barely heard it.

"Frost?"

It was Bess's voice. He opened his eye—the light outside the window was gray and he looked at the luminous black face of the Rolex, uncoiling his left arm from around Bess's shoulder to do so. It was almost seven A.M.

"That the alarm?"

"It's the phone."

"It is the phone—yeah—I knew that," he muttered, throwing his feet over the bed.

"Here—it's right here." The ringing stopped and he sat back on the bed, taking the receiver from her hand as she set the telephone carriage on the bed between them.

"Hello," he coughed into the telephone. It was Mike O'Hara. Arika Gorki had been traced. There'd be a car outside for Frost in twenty minutes.

Frost hung up the phone, then leaned across Bess to kiss her. "Tell Mike hello," she whispered. "And don't get killed."

"I'll go along with that," the one-eyed man nodded.

Chapter Thirty

Frost was warm. The car's engine was off and the Charleston, South Carolina, temperature was warm enough that air-conditioning was necessary. He would have liked to have removed his suit jacket, but then the Cobra Gunskin rig with the Metalifed High Power in it would have shown and one of the people walking the cobbled streets of the historic district could have looked into the car and seen a man with a gun. A scream, a shout, a call to the police—any of that might alert Arika Gorki. She was traveling with a man. O'Hara, sitting in the front seat opposite the driver, had said the man was assumed to be Serge Leontovitch, himself KGB, a troubleshooter for them. In a way, Frost almost wished Leontovitch were literally a "troubleshooter"—someone who would shoot Arika Gorki, a woman who had been nothing but trouble.

"They're stayin' there under assumed names. She's got her hair dyed blonde—or maybe it's a wig. I dunno. No passports under either name. My guess is they got some private pilot lined up to take 'em for a ride and they'll hijack him to Cuba or somethin'," O'Hara suddenly observed.

"How about him?"

"Carries a Walther P-38—supposed to be pretty good with it. At least six kills we know of, probably three or four times that many we don't know about. They sent him in to get her out. He's a top gun for 'em."

"How'd you connive me in on this?"

"I reminded the guys at the Bureau what a wonderful sport you'd been not goin' to the papers, not havin' Bess do it—nothing about your little trip to Russia at all. But don't go shootin' anybody less you have to. The Bureau might holler at me."

"I want her—dead or alive doesn't matter, so long as she won't be repatriated or traded off."

"No, Uncle Sam gets her and she's in the slam until she rots. Good place for her, too."

"You don't believe that any more than I do—about her stayin' in the slam," Frost remarked matter-of-factly, staring out the window, lighting a cigarette.

"I don't think there'll be any shooting at all," the driver's voice offered.

Frost looked at him. "What? They're just gonna surrender when you guys shout 'FBI' at 'em? Bullshit."

"Frost is right, Ferguson. Those kinds of people don't give up. Unless we pin 'em down in one spot, all the exits cut, plenty of cops visible and no potential hostages or anything for them to take, then we've got a gunfight. So if we do, we gotta make it fast before some of these tourists get hurt."

It was Ferguson's voice again, Frost still watching the street. "The local police have the building surrounded—a lot of those tourists aren't. In—" Ferguson paused, Frost guessed to look at a wristwatch. "—in two minutes almost exactly. I step out of the car, aim my bullhorn at the parking lot and we close in."

"They always come to the car at exactly seven o'clock?" Frost glanced at his Rolex.

"They have for the last three nights in a row. Then

they drive out toward the islands—out by James Island and Folly Beach, find some place for dinner, get back to their room around ten or eleven."

"Why haven't you nailed 'em sooner?" Frost asked.

"First night, off-duty Charleston police officer spotted them, figured it was the Gorki woman despite the hair, and by the time he could get to a car, it was too late to follow 'em," Ferguson said. "We staked out the hotel, got a warrant and checked the rooms. It was them. Second night, we tailed them all the way. Found out they were just going out to eat and let them go back to the hotel unmolested. Figured maybe we could find their local contacts, get their escape route figured, whatever. All they did was goof off all day long. Maybe tonight's the night."

"For the escape?" Frost murmured noncommittally. "Maybe. If not, then soon. They're setting up a pattern. Different restaurant each night. One of these nights, they'll slip out on you, then bye-bye."

"I don't think they've been alerted to our surveillance."

Frost nodded absently, "I'll buy that—you guys did a good job, looks like. Otherwise," and he laughed, "they wouldn't be walking to that parking lot right now."

Frost didn't move, didn't turn his head, barely dared to shift his gaze behind the dark sunglasses.

"Hello, Arika baby," O'Hara murmured.

Ferguson hit a walkie-talkie button, there was the crackle of static, then, "This is Ferguson—delay closing in until I give the signal. The subjects are proceeding into the parking lot from the main entrance. The man is wearing a sportcoat and the women is carrying the large handbag—assume both to be armed. Approach with caution. Ferguson out."

The one-eyed man reached under his jacket, tempted as they passed by the car simply to step out onto the curb and put a bullet in the back of her head. The hell with the man, he thought. Tempted—but he didn't.

He ripped the customized Metalifed High Power from the leather, the hammer already cocked, the built-up safety locked.

He heard the sound of metal against leather, then the sound of a cylinder being rolled then rocked back into its frame. It would be O'Hara with the big Model 29 .44 Mag six-inch.

"Too bad there's only two of 'em," O'Hara's voice whispered.

"Two's enough," Frost whispered back.

"Gentlemen, this is an arrest, not a vendetta," Ferguson said. Frost glanced at him, noticing the younger man's tightly clenched teeth and forced smile.

"For you it's an arrest," Frost said.

O'Hara finished it. "For him and me—it's a vendetta. I got the scars to prove it."

They turned into the parking lot. Arika looked lovely despite the unreal blonde hair, a midcalf-length skirt that looked to be wool covering the tops of high heeled boots, a black turtleneck sweater, and a stole made from the same material wrapped around her shoulders. The black bag hanging from her left shoulder looked heavy. Frost wondered what was inside it.

The man with her—Leontovitch—was shorter than she was, at least with the heels she wore, and slightly built with long-fingered hands swinging easily at his sides. He wore a tweed sportcoat and gray slacks, his shoes immaculately shined. The tweed sportcoat could easily hide a gun as large as a P-38.

"What's Arika like to carry—anybody know?" Frost asked anyone listening.

Ferguson answered, "Miss Gorki habitually carries a Smith & Wesson Model 19 .357 Magnum with four-inch barrel and a lockblade folding knife—or at least she did when she was in the—er— They're ready to get into the car."

Frost laughed. Ferguson didn't even want to say "CIA."

"I'd say don't get out of the car, Mr. Ferguson," Frost advised. "Use the bullhorn from cover."

"No—but thanks for the advice." Ferguson opened the door, stepping onto the curb.

O'Hara rasped, "Oh, boy."

Frost dropped the safety on the Metalifed High Power.

His ears vibrated with the sound of the bullhorn. "Arika Ladislava Gorki and Serge Aritide Leontovitch—we have Federal and local warrants for your arrest. Raise your hands over your heads. This is the—"

Ferguson didn't get to say "FBI." Frost saw the black shape of the P-38 in Leontovitch's right hand, started to shout to Ferguson, but the bullet had ripped through the shell of the bullhorn, slamming it up into Ferguson's face. Ferguson sprawled across the hood of the F.O.U.O. Plymouth, his mouth gushing blood.

"I'll help Ferguson!" O'Hara was shouting as Frost rolled out the doorway and onto the curb. The rear door of the Plymouth opened wide for cover as the one-eyed man snapped the High Power over the door frame and fired.

Leontovitch was dropping behind the car he and Arika had been opening, the heavier sounds of Arika's .357 Magnum booming as a wave of uniformed police ran from cover in the front of the church that owned the parking lot. Frost snapped off two shots from the High Power, Arika's fire apparently directed toward the police. One of the uniformed officers went down.

"I got him!" It was O'Hara shouting. That he'd gotten Ferguson to safety? "I got Ferguson, Frost!"

In the next instant, Frost heard the cannonlike boom

of O'Hara's .44 Magnum, Frost deciding he was just at the right spot for maximum effect to his hearing from the recoil. 180-grain JHPs.

"There's another bullhorn in the trunk!" O'Hara shouted.

"The hell with it," Frost shouted back.

As he spoke, he saw a uniformed Charleston police officer silhouetted against the church doorway, a bullhorn already in hand, "This is the police," the voice boomed. "Lay down your weapons! We have you—!"

There was a boom from behind the car, a tongue of orange flame licking out. She had to be firing 125-grain JHPs for muzzle flash like that, Frost decided. The police officer ducked back into the doorway.

There was a burst of gunfire, half sounding like the 9mm Walther P-38 Leontovitch had, half from the .357 Magnum, both from behind the car. Police gunfire hammered toward the position. Frost saw it before he heard it—the belch of gray smoke from the automobile's exhaust. Arika was up, the blonde hair blowing in the slight breeze, the revolver belching fire in her hands as she dove into the car. The car was already in motion, high speed reversing, flick-turning, then driving across the far sidewalk.

"Holy—"

"Nuts," Frost shouted back. The one-eyed man was to his feet, firing the High Power toward the car's rear windshield as it crashed through the line of uniformed police and plainclothesmen coming up on the position from behind. There was the boom of a riot shotgun, the rattle of an M-16, but the car was gone.

"Son of a—"

Frost threw himself behind the wheel of the F.O.U.O. Plymouth, not finishing the epithet.

"Wait for me," O'Hara was shouting. Frost was already firing the engine and throwing the selector into drive. He stomped the gas pedal, cutting the wheel into a sharp right from the curb and into the street, O'Hara slamming the door.

"Jees—this brass is hot," O'Hara snapped, dumping the 29's cylinder, then ramming a Safariland speed-loader against it as Frost shot a glance toward him.

"Yeah, tell me about it!" The one-eyed man cut the wheel hard left, across the sidewalk past the police milling on the street, past the police car coming to block the intersection. "Get on the radio, Mike—find out where the hell they're headin'."

The one-eyed man braced himself, the Plymouth bouncing the curb onto the street as he cut the wheel hard left, in the direction they'd taken.

"Got a black and white—or whatever color they are here—picked 'em up. Sounds like two blocks down on the left."

"Gotcha," Frost snapped, cutting the wheel left, across another curb. The right front fender shagged a trash can as Frost turned up an alley and started to accelerate.

"Ferguson told me a lot of these are—"

"Hell," Frost rasped. The alley was a dead end. But there was a yard, ornately landscaped, a fountain bubbling at its center, a low wooden fence protecting it. And beyond the yard was the street. Frost stomped the brakes, cutting the wheel sharp right and through the fence, accelerating.

"They're gonna kill you for this," O'Hara winced.

"Pickey pickey," Frost laughed. He was having the time of his life. And he missed the fountain by a good six inches he judged.

"That's probably a landmark, Frost—"

Frost didn't pay attention, bouncing the car over the curb and onto the street between a horse carriage and a Volkswagen, cutting a sharp left and recovering it into a hard right at the next intersection. There was a traffic light ahead, going red and Frost shouted, "There a siren on this thing?"

"Yeah."

"Hit it, Mike!"

Frost worked the horn buttons, the traffic at the intersection slowing. Then as the siren came on the cars peeled away, Frost threading the needle of stopped cars, making a hard left and then accelerating.

"This is O'Hara. I'm in Ferguson's car. Where's the Gorki woman and Leontovitch? We're moving down—never mind. O'Hara out." And O'Hara rasped, "There they are."

Frost could see the yellow car ahead of him, cutting left to avoid a police car. The siren wailing deafeningly, Frost made the same sharp left, accelerating past the police car now pursuing the yellow car. "Can't shoot," O'Hara was shouting. "Too many innocent people around."

Almost as if they'd heard O'Hara, gunfire came from the yellow car. Frost swerved as the upper left corner of the windshield spiderwebbed. "I hate it when people shoot glass all over me," the one-eyed man snapped, watching as the yellow car—cut off again—took another sharp left. "There's that market section over there. They can't get a car through it very easily," Frost shouted.

"Betcha they'll try though," O'Hara called back. The yellow car accelerated now, sidewiping a motorcycle, sending the rider sprawling, then passing through another intersection. The street was cobbled and Frost could feel the bumps and jars, the constant shuddering, and the sponginess of the steering. He fought the wheel, cutting a wide arc around the injured cyclist, then accelerating again, sideswiping a trash can. He bounced across the narrow street, sideswiping a boat trailer, then bouncing back, straightening out and accelerating again.

"You drive like you're crazy—you talk about the way I drive," O'Hara almost screamed.

The one-eyed man watched the yellow car. It cut a sharp right, fishtailing right ahead of him. Frost made the turn then less than fifty yards behind it, stomping the brakes, the car skidding. The market section was crowded. Black women were selling baskets from the curb stones; the center of the section itself was like a long, narrow shopping mall, a cobbled street flanking it. Pedestrians crowded back against the curbs now as Frost pulled the F.O.U.O. Plymouth to a bouncing halt behind the yellow car. He jumped out, O'Hara already onto the curb, the big .44 Magnum held out ahead of him.

"Out of the way—out of the way—FBI!" O'Hara crouched behind the rear deck of the yellow rental car, Frost already in a crouch on the street side of it. The High Power, one of the twenty-round extension magazines loaded, was in both Frost's fists.

It was a woman's voice that screamed it. "They hit that lamp post, then they ran down the street."

Frost looked at her, then approached the car. There was no sign of injury to either Arika Gorki or Leontovitch in the car. "Shit!" He started to run, hearing O'Hara shout a thank you to the woman bystander. O'Hara was outdistancing him, Frost's left leg still paining him slightly. O'Hara skidded to a halt on his heels as they entered the long market mall beyond the first block. Stalls selling everything from jewelry to clothing to sea shells were lined on both sides and ranked down the middle—and in the center of the stalls, there was a knot of humanity, moving backward slowly, as if someone in front of them were pushing them back.

"I think this is it!" O'Hara shouted.

"Take the far side. I'll come up the middle," Frost ordered, glancing once to O'Hara who was already moving out.

Frost shoved his way through the crowd, people screaming as they saw his gun. "I'm with the police," Frost shouted. It was partially true. He glanced behind him; more than a dozen uniformed officers were in the market mall now, threading their way through the crowd.

Frost kept pushing his way forward, then stopped. Arika Gorki, the blonde hair gone, the wig apparently discarded, her black hair pulled up tight, close to her head, held a frail-looking old woman in front of her. The gun in Arika's hand was held at the right side of the woman's head.

"Give it up, Arika," Frost shouted. "You don't kill anybody, all they'll do is deport you!"

"Go to hell, Frost," she screamed.

And then Frost saw Leontovitch, pulling a group of children around him to use as a shield, the Walther P-38 in his right fist. His left fist was knotted in the hair of a beautiful little girl looking no more than ten. The little girl screamed, tears streaming down her cheeks.

"I want all the police out of here," Leontovitch shouted. "Or this little girl and all these children—I'll kill them."

"No!" Frost shouted it, feeling the word rising out of him like an impulse from his subconscious. "No, you son of a bitch!"

"I'll back ya," Frost heard O'Hara shout.

Frost raised the pistol in his hands, aiming it slowly at Leontovitch's head.

"Let go of the little girl or you're dead." Frost stared at him. "Here and now—you're dead, you sucker!" Then, to O'Hara, "Mike, settle that .44 right on the other side of his head there—we'll blow his brains all over the market!"

"Arika!" It was Leontovitch shouting.

"Forget it," Frost shouted. "Arika's not gonna drop her shield to help you out. You're on your own, asshole! Now let go of the girl and drop the gun or I'll shoot and so will O'Hara." Frost shouted over his right shoulder. "Mike, count of three—pop him. One!"

"Arika!" Leontovitch's scream was barely human.

"Two!" It was O'Hara who shouted it.

Frost settled the built-up sights of the High Power in the bridge of Leontovitch's nose.

Leontovitch let loose of the girl and started to run, Frost shouting, "Everybody hit the floor."

Leontovitch was running hard, straight down the center of the market. Frost heard the light, popping sound of his 9mm, a rapid, two-shot burst. The sound died in the massive booming of O'Hara's .44. Leontovitch's body stumbled forward; then, the .44 doing its work, the body backflipped across a stall filled with sea shells.

There was a man's voice—Frost didn't know if it were a cop or one of the bystanders. "She's getting away! The woman is getting away!"

Frost wheeled left, swinging the High Power's muzzle with his body motion. The old woman was on the floor of the market stalls. Arika, the shawl hanging at a crazy angle across her back, was running out the far side of the market.

"Goin' after her," Frost shouted, then started to run. His leg ached—the hell with it, he thought.

He hit the end of the mall, hung right and ran, shouting after her, "Arika!"

She turned, dodging into the protection of a doorway across the street, firing. Frost dropped into the street, hearing a scream behind him as the bullet must have met a target. Frost—firing at an upward angle—pumped the High Power's trigger, again and again, seeing the chips of masonry and brick scattering under the impact of the bullets as he pinned her back.

He caught her silhouette for a split second, bringing the High Power around to it. But the .357 in her hands barked twice, one of the cobble stones beside Frost's head powdering under the impact of a slug, fragments of stone powdering Frost's face. He pushed himself to his feet again, running, Arika ahead of him. As he ran, Frost dumped the partially spent magazine, replacing it with the second twenty-rounder that he'd stuffed in his belt. Arika was outdistancing him despite the high-heeled boots she wore.

Ahead, Frost caught sight of a railing, the street opening out on the left toward the sea. There was a blob of gray far out in the harbor—it was Ft. Sumter. He'd read you could see it from the Battery. Arika was running along the railing now, then turned, firing the .357 Magnum. Frost threw himself down to the cobbled street, firing a succession of two-round bursts toward her. Looking up, Arika was gone.

"Hell," he rasped, pushing himself to his feet, running.

He reached the railing, then looked over the side. There was a shell-strewn spot of beach beyond the railing, which during high tide, he realized, would be swamped. He pushed himself up, then flipped the railing to the sand below, coming down hard, his left leg paining him. He could hear O'Hara's voice shouting from somewhere behind him, but he didn't bother to answer.

Half stumbling on the sea shells, he dropped into a classic combat crouch, the High Power in both fists. "Arika!"

She wheeled, firing. Frost fired simultaneously. She

spun, falling, and Frost started to run toward her. She was up again, the revolver in her right hand, but nothing was coming from it as Frost threw himself to the sand.

He stood up, the revolver dropping to the sand beside her, her left arm limp at her side. Her black sweater and the plaid skirt and the black boots were covered with grains of sand.

She dropped the shoulder bag she'd worn, the shawl slipping from her shoulders. In her right hand, she held the lock-bladed folding knife she was known to carry.

"Give it up," Frost snapped.

"Kill me—if you can," she shrieked.

"Give it up!"

"That old woman who helped you. As soon as I got to a courier, I gave the KGB the location of her farm. They arrested her husband. They shot her!"

"All right," Frost said calmly. He raised the High Power in his right hand and pulled the trigger once. There was a hole like a third eye in the middle of the bridge of her nose, and her body fell straight back into the sand. She flopped for a second like a fish out of water on the beach, and then she was still.

The one-eyed man upped the Metalifed High Power's safety, then shoved the gun into his belt. In his left pocket he found his cigarettes, then lit one in the blue-yellow flame of the lighter.

The sand would ruin his suit, but it was ruined anyway. And the sixty-five dollar shoes were covered with it.

He sat down among the sea shells. The shells, however beautiful, were reminders of the death which brought them here. And he waited for O'Hara and the police. The woman beside him lingered in his memory. But the ocean looked very calm.

THE SURVIVALIST SERIES
by Jerry Ahern

#1: TOTAL WAR (960, $2.50)
The first in the shocking series that follows the unrelenting search for ex-CIA covert operations officer John Thomas Rourke to locate his missing family—after the button is pressed, the missiles launched and the multimegaton bombs unleashed . . .

#2: THE NIGHTMARE BEGINS (810, $2.50)
After WW III, the United States is just a memory. But ex-CIA covert operations officer Rourke hasn't forgotten his family. While hiding from the Soviet occupation forces, he adheres to his search!

#3: THE QUEST (851, $2.50)
Not even a deadly game of intrigue within the Soviet High Command, the formation of the American "resistance" and a highly placed traitor in the new U.S. government can deter Rourke from continuing his desperate search for his family.

#4: THE DOOMSAYER (893, $2.50)
The most massive earthquake in history is only hours away, and Communist-Cuban troops, Soviet-Cuban rivalry, and a traitor in the inner circle of U.S. II block Rourke's path. But he must go on—he is THE SURVIVALIST.

#5: THE WEB (1145, $2.50)
Blizzards rage around Rourke as he picks up the trail of his family and is forced to take shelter in a strangely quiet Tennessee valley town. Things seem too normal here, as if no one has heard of the War; but the quiet isn't going to last for long!

AND DON'T FORGET TO READ . . .

THE SCOUT BY BUCK GENTRY

#1: ROWAN'S RAIDERS (754, $2.50)

Six years in the camps of the fierce, savage Oglala Sioux trained Eli Holten to be an expert in hunting, tracking—and killing. Now, as an Army wagon commander in the wilderness, the Scout rides each danger-filled mile as if it were his last . . .

#2: DAKOTA MASSACRE (794, $2.50)

After a brutal Sioux surprise attack, Eli Holten's instincts tell him the massacre was too much a surprise. And the Scout won't take things lying down!

#6: BANDIT FURY (1075, $2.50)

Through the vast, snow-covered Dakota Plains to the Deadwood and the Black Hills, the Scout maneuvers his way on the bloody path of a fast trigger—and into the soft, warm valleys of his luscious companion!

BOLT BY CORT MARTIN

#9: BADMAN'S BORDELLO (1127, $2.25)

When the women of Cheyenne cross the local hardcases to exercise their right to vote, Bolt discovers that politics makes for strange bedfellows!

#10: BAWDY HOUSE SHOWDOWN (1176, $2.25)

The best man to run the new brothel in San Francisco is Bolt. But Bolt's intimate interviews lead to a shoot-out that has the city quaking—and the girls shaking!

#11: THE LAST BORDELLO (1224, $2.25)

A working girl in Angel's camp doesn't stand a chance—unless Jared Bolt takes up arms to bring a little peace to the town . . . and discovers that the trouble is caused by a woman who used to do the same!

Available wherever paperbacks are sold, or order direct from the Publisher. Send cover price plus 50¢ per copy for mailing and handling to Zebra Books, 475 Park Avenue South, New York, N.Y. 10016 DO NOT SEND CASH.

"SPACE GHOST!"

Eril dredged his memory for anything he could remember about this phenomenon. "They're sighted along the old interstellar routes. There're only about six or seven documented cases known, never this close to a planet. They probably don't actually exist in three-space."

As Eril spoke, the figure descended until its feet seemed to touch the tunnel floor. For a moment it stood there, motionless. Then it began to move toward them, drifting along in a mechanical parody of walking.

"Whatever you are," Kithri called out, "you stay away from my ship!"

"There's no danger. The ghost can't interact with ordinary matter," Eril said with a confidence he did not feel. "There's nothing to worry about. It'll dematerialize in a moment."

But the ghost kept coming, and it was not moving toward them but toward Kithri's scrubjet. Now it was close enough to the scrubjet to touch it. The ghost stretched out one thick-fingered hand, now clearly visible as it took on greater and greater solidity.

"No!" Kithri screamed, and lunged for the scrubjet. . . .